Edward Bean Underhill

The Tragedy of Morant Bay

A Narrative of the Distrubances in the Island of Jamaica in 1865

Edward Bean Underhill

The Tragedy of Morant Bay
A Narrative of the Distrubances in the Island of Jamaica in 1865

ISBN/EAN: 9783743403291

Manufactured in Europe, USA, Canada, Australia, Japa

Cover: Foto ©Raphael Reischuk / pixelio.de

Manufactured and distributed by brebook publishing software (www.brebook.com)

Edward Bean Underhill

The Tragedy of Morant Bay

THE

TRAGEDY OF MORANT BAY

A NARRATIVE

OF THE

DISTURBANCES IN THE ISLAND OF JAMAICA

IN

1865

BY

EDWARD BEAN UNDERHILL, LL.D.

(Honorary Secretary of the Baptist Missionary Society).

London:

ALEXANDER & SHEPHEARD, FURNIVAL ST., HOLBORN

1895

LONDON :

PRINTED BY ALEXANDER AND SHEPHEARD,

27, CHANCERY LANE, W.C.

PREFACE.

THE following narrative owes its existence to the earnest desire of my family, and other friends, to possess an authentic account of the events, antecedent and consequent, to the Disturbances which took place at Morant Bay, in the Island of Jamaica, in the month of October, 1865. This desire I have endeavoured to gratify.

My concern with the "Tragedy" will be found sufficiently explained in the Introduction and in the narrative itself. My personal recollections I have tested and supported by reference to public documents; but I am especially indebted to the suggestions and manuscript reminiscences of my dear friend, the Rev. D. J. East, for more than forty years a resident in the Island, and President of Calabar College, Kingston. I have also, in various parts, availed myself of papers and communications published by me in the periodicals of the time.

HAMPSTEAD,
  February, 1895.

CONTENTS.

CHAPTER XIV.

CHAPTER XV.

CHAPTER XVI.

INTRODUCTION.

L ETTERS from the missionaries of the Baptist Missionary Society, in the year 1864, brought vividly to the attention of the Committee the depression existing throughout the Island of Jamaica, among every section of the community engaged in agriculture and mercantile pursuits. The returns from the churches revealed a state of poverty of the most distressing kind, more serious than the island had for many years experienced, attributable in part to the long and severe drought of more than two years' duration. It was followed by widespread sick-ness. To the great decay of the sugar cultivation, and the low price of produce, were added the dear-ness of apparel, and a growing diminution in the wages of the labouring population. Schools and churches fell off in attendance, and crime was largely on the increase. The reports from ministers of other missionary bodies were fully confirmatory of this state of things.

An eye-witness thus describes what was passing around him:—"There was hardly any employment for labourers on the sugar estates, through the failure of crops. The provision grounds of the people scarcely afforded any subsistence. For food, such as corn-meal and flour, all classes were mostly dependent on supplies from abroad. To obtain it the poor had to run into debt at the stores, thus entailing difficulties which for years crippled their resources. I have seen men and women with looks of despair, having neither food nor clothing for themselves or their children. I have preached in chapels partly deserted, in which not a child was to be seen, because parents could not find them food or raiment. In some districts, the mango tree supplied the only food of the inhabitants. Oh! it was a time of despair and woe to both ministers and their flocks; and, but for the response of British Christians to appeals made on their behalf, multitudes must have perished." *

For the relief of this painful state of things, the Baptist churches of Great Britain, at the call of the Baptist Missionary Society, raised at once a sum of £1,500, and as the distress deepened, early in 1865, added to their donations a further sum of £2,500, for the special needs of the pastors and their congregations.

No relief was forthcoming from the Government or Legislature of the Colony. The administration of justice was felt to be partial and often unjust. The governing classes were indifferent and venal. Laws, oppressive and injurious in their operation on the emancipated population, were the fruit of the

* "Reminiscences of the Rev. D. J. East," p. 9 (M.S.).

dominant influence of the planting interest in the Legislature, to which the improved education of the people rendered them more sensitive. They were more than observant of the increased taxation, of the increased expenditure, and of the increased punishment rendered necessary by the growth of crime. Starvation is ever a soil most fertile in discontent, and a spirit of restlessness began everywhere to appear.

Being on a visit to Sir Morton Peto, M.P., Treasurer of the Baptist Missionary Society, at Christmastide, 1864, these distressing communications were naturally a frequent topic of conversation between us. Returning with him to town, our minds sorely burdened with the sad tidings which every mail disclosed, he warmly approved my suggestion that I should bring the case to the notice of the Right Honourable E. Cardwell, then Secretary of State for the Colonies.

I may here mention that through my father, who, with my brother, had given Mr. Cardwell valued assistance at a General Election, I was introduced to that gentleman, and had received the kind permission to write him on any matter on which he could afford me assistance. My father had also sent Mr. Cardwell a copy of my work on the " Social and Religious Condition of the West Indies," published in 1862. In reply to this, Mr. Cardwell said that he had always taken a deep interest in the question of emancipation, though he was not without some doubts " whether the measures actually adopted were in all respects

perfectly adapted and most **conducive to the interests
of the negro."** *

This also **had** been the emphatic opinion of his predecessor, **Earl Grey, who** held that the negro part of
the Jamaica **population did not, by its** voting power,
exercise such an **influence over the** Legislature as to
exempt **the advisers of the Crown from the** duty of
keeping a watchful eye upon the proceedings of the
Legislature, **for the** purpose of **checking any** attempt
which might be made to pass **laws bearing** unfairly
on the labouring classes.   Unfortunately the English
Government had occasion too frequently to express
their disapproval of Acts of the Jamaica Legislature,
and to refuse **to them the Royal Assent.†**

On reaching home I devoted myself to the pre-
paration of the letter to which subsequent events
have given **so much importance.   It** was despatched
**to Mr. Cardwell, under cover from Sir Morton Peto,
on the 5th January, 1865.   In** a **few days, on the** 27th,
its reception was acknowledged, with **the information**
that the letter had **been** forwarded **to the Governor of**
Jamaica with instructions **to** report on its contents.

As this letter is **the subject** of many references in
the following **pages, I append a** copy of **it for the full
information of my readers.‡**

---

* **Letter dated from 74,** Eaton Square, **February 11th,
1862.**

† Earl Grey on " The Colonial Policy of Lord John Russell's
Administration," vol. 1, p. 24.

‡ " Papers on the Affairs of **Jamaica, presented to** Parliament, February, 1866," pp. 1 to 3.

Letter from E. B. Underhill, Esq., LL.D., to the Right Hon. Edward Cardwell, M.P.

" 33, Moorgate Street, E.C.,
" 5th January, 1865.

" Dear Sir,—I venture to ask your kind consideration of a few observations on the present condition of the Island of Jamaica.

" For several months past, every mail has brought letters informing me of the continually increasing distress of the coloured population. As a sufficient illustration I quote the following brief passage from one of them :—

" ' Crime has fearfully increased. The number of prisoners in the penitentiary and gaols is considerably more than double the average, and nearly all for one crime—larceny. Summonses for petty debts disclose an amount of pecuniary difficulty which has never before been experienced, and applications for parochial and private relief prove that multitudes are suffering from want little removed from starvation.'

" The immediate cause of this distress would seem to be the drought of the last two years; but, in fact, this has only given intensity to suffering previously existing. All accounts, both public and private, concur in affirming the alarming increase of crime, chiefly of larceny and petty theft. This arises from the extreme poverty of the people. That this is its true origin is made evident by the ragged and even naked condition of vast numbers of them; so contrary to the taste for dress they usually exhibit. They cannot purchase clothing, partly from its greatly increased cost, which is unduly enhanced by the duty (said to be thirty-eight per cent. by the Honourable Mr. Whitelock), which it now pays, and partly from the want of employment and the consequent absence of wages.

" The people, then, are starving, and the causes of this are not far to seek. No doubt the taxation of the island is too heavy for its present resources, and must necessarily render the cost of producing the staples higher than they can bear to meet competition in the markets of the world. No doubt much of the sugar-land of the island is worn out, or can only be made productive by an outlay which would destroy all hope of profitable return. No doubt, too, a large part of the island is uncultivated, and might be made to support a vastly greater population than is now existing upon it.

" But the simple fact is, there is not sufficient employment for the people; there is neither work for them, nor the capital to employ them.

" The labouring class is too numerous for the work to be done. Sugar cultivation on the estates does not absorb more than 30,000 of the people, and every other species of cultivation (apart from provision growing) cannot give employment to more than another 30,000. But the agricultural population of the island is over 400,000, so that there are at least 340,000 persons whose livelihood depends on employment other than that devoted to the staple cultivation of the island. Of these 340,000 certainly not less than 130,000 are adults and capable of labour. For subsistence they must be entirely dependent on the provisions grown on their little freeholds, a portion of which is sold to those who find employment on the estates, or, perhaps, in a slight degree, on such produce as they are able to raise for exportation. But those who grow produce for exportation are very few, and they meet with every kind of discouragement to prosecute a means of support which is as advantageous to the island as to themselves. If their provisions fail, as has been the case, from drought, they must steal or starve. And this is their present condition.

"The same result follows in this country, when employment ceases or wages fail. The great decrease of coin in circulation in Jamaica is a further proof that less money is spent in wages through the decline of employment. Were Jamaica prosperous, silver would flow into it, or its equivalent in English manufactures, instead of the exportation of silver, which now regularly takes place. And if, as stated in the Governor's speech, the Customs revenue in the year gone by has been equal to former years, this has arisen, not from an increase in the quantities imported, but from the increased value of the imports, the duty being levied at an *ad valorem* charge of $12\frac{1}{2}$ per cent. on articles, such as cotton goods, which have, within the last year or two, greatly risen in price.

"I shall say nothing of the course taken by the Jamaica Legislature; of their abortive Immigration Bills; of their unjust taxation of the coloured population; of their refusal of just tribunals; of their

denial of political rights to the emancipated negroes.
Could the people find remunerative employment,
these evils would, in time, be remedied from their
growing strength and intelligence. The worst evil
consequent on the proceedings of the Legislature is
the distrust awakened in the minds of capitalists, and
the avoidance of Jamaica, with its manifold advantages, by all who possess the means to benefit it by
their expenditure. Unless means can be found to
encourage the outlay of capital in Jamaica in the
growth of those numerous products which can be
profitably exported, so that employment can be given
to its starving people, I see no other result than the
entire failure of the island, and the destruction of the
hopes that the Legislature and the people of Great
Britain have cherished with regard to the well-being
of its emancipated population.

"With your kind permission, I will venture to
make two or three suggestions which, if carried out,
may assist to avert so painful a result.

"1. A searching inquiry into the legislation of the
island since emancipation—its taxation, its economical
and material condition—would go far to bring to
light the causes of the existing evils, and, by convinc-
ing the ruling class of the mistakes of the past, lead
to their removal. Such an inquiry seems also due to
this country, that it may be seen whether the emancipated peasantry have gained those advantages which
were sought to be secured to them by their enfran-
chisement.

"2. The Governor might be instructed to encourage

by his personal approval and urgent recommendation the growth of exportable produce by the people on the very numerous freeholds they possess. This might be done by the formation of associations for shipping their produce in considerable quantities; by equalising duties on the produce of the people and that of the planting interests; by instructing the native growers of produce in the best methods of cultivation, and by pointing out the articles which would find a ready sale in the markets of the world; by opening channels for direct transmission of produce, without the intervention of agents, from whose extortions and frauds the people now frequently suffer and are greatly discouraged. The cultivation of sugar by the peasantry should, in my judgment, be discouraged. At the best, with all the scientific appliances the planters can bring to it, both of capital and machinery, sugar manufacturing is a hazardous thing. Much more must it become so in the hands of the people, with their rude mills and imperfect methods. But the minor products of the island, such as spices, tobacco, farinaceous foods, coffee, and cotton, are quite within their reach, and always fetch a fair and remunerative price where not burdened by extravagant charges and local taxation.

"3. With just laws and light taxation, capitalists would be encouraged to settle in Jamaica, and employ themselves in the production of the more important staples, such as sugar, coffee, and cotton. Thus the people would be employed, and the present starvation rate of wages be improved.

"In conclusion, I have to apologise for troubling you with this communication; but since my visit to the island in 1859-60, I have felt the greatest interest in its prosperity, and deeply grieve over the sufferings of its coloured population. It is more than time that the unwisdom—to use the gentlest term—that has governed Jamaica since emancipation should be brought to an end; a course of action which, while it incalculably aggravates the misery arising from natural, and, therefore, unavoidable, causes, renders certain the ultimate ruin of every class-planter and peasant, European and creole.

"Should you, dear Sir, desire such information as it may be in my power to furnish, or to see me on the matter, I shall be most happy either to forward whatever facts I may possess or wait upon you at any time that you may appoint.

"I have, etc.,

(*Signed*) "EDWARD B. UNDERHILL.

"P.S.—I append an extract from the speech of the Hon. H. A. Whitelock, in the House of Assembly, with respect to the condition of the people.

"'He (Mr. Whitelock) would make an assertion which could not be gainsaid by his successor, that taxation could not be extended; not one farthing more could be imposed on the people, who were suffering peculiar hardship from the increased value of wearing apparel, which was now taxed beyond all bounds. Actually, they were paying 38 per cent.

now, when 12½ per cent. was before considered an outrageous *ad valorem* duty. Cotton goods, including Oznaburgh, and all the wearing apparel of the labouring classes had increased 200 per cent. in value. What was bought at 4d. per yard before was selling at a shilling per yard. Therefore, the people are now paying 1½d. duty on every yard of cloth, instead of one halfpenny, which has been justly described as a heavy impost. The consequence is that a disgusting state of nudity exhibited itself in some parts of the country. Hardly a boy under ten years of age wore a frock; and adults, from the ragged state of their garments, exhibited those parts of the body where covering was especially wanted. The lower classes hitherto exhibited a proneness for dress, and he could not believe such a change would have come over them but for his belief in their destitution, arising out of a reduction in their wages at a time when every article of apparel had risen in value. This year's decrease in imports foreshadowed what was coming. Sugar was down again at £11 per hogshead; coffee was falling; pimento was valueless; logwood was scarcely worth cutting; and, moreover, a sad diminution was effected in our chief staple exports from a deficiency of rain.' "

It will now be my object to trace, as impartially and truthfully as I can, the origin and course of those stirring events which arose from the steps taken by the Secretary of State for the Colonies.

THE TRAGEDY OF MORANT BAY.

CHAPTER I.

THE CONDITION OF JAMAICA.

I VISITED the Island of Jamaica, in company with the Rev. J. T. Brown, of Northampton, as a Deputation from the Baptist Missionary Society, in the cold season of 1859-60. After a short sojourn in Trinidad and in Haiti, I landed in Kingston on the 5th November, and proceeded, with my colleague, on his arrival a few days later, to visit nearly every part of the island, inquiring into the religious and social condition of the people. We concluded our investigations on the 9th April, when I left in order to inspect the stations of the Society in the Bahamas. Captain Darling was at that time the Governor of Jamaica. On account of ill-health he was compelled to seek leave of absence at the close of the year 1861.

In the early part of 1862, Edward John Eyre, Esq., some time Lieutenant-Governor of Antigua, was selected by the Duke of Newcastle, then Colonial Secretary of State, to succeed Captain Darling, as Lieutenant-Governor, and in May, 1864, he received full powers to act as Captain-General and Governor of the island.

1

The first measure of Mr. Eyre brought him a considerable amount of popularity, especially among the missionaries of all denominations. Its object was to secure men of good and pure character for public appointments. Intemperate or immoral habits were held to be a bar to office. Though warmly approved by the moral and religious portion of the people, it stirred up the anger of other classes, so that on meeting his first Assembly in November he found himself in the presence of an active and influential opposition. In carrying out his well-intentioned purpose he had unwittingly aroused the susceptibilities of many persons, and touched a sore spot in the body corporate. Early in the month of October, 1862, we find the Duke of Newcastle addressing a reproof to Mr. Eyre for reflections, in his despatches, upon the private character of certain persons who had attended a public meeting held in favour of Mr. G. W. Gordon. "I feel sure," says the Duke of Newcastle, "that you will find it most conducive to the public interests you have at heart, to occupy yourself rather with the substance of acts and proceedings with which you have to deal, than with the private characters of the persons who may assail or defend them." *

In entering on his duties, there can be no question that Mr. Eyre was actuated by the best of motives, but he soon found himself unequal to the strife, under conditions many of which were the fatal heritage of the errors of the past. The constitution of the Govern-

* Blue Book on Gordon's Removal from the Commission of the Peace. Returned 2nd March, 1866, p. 41.

ment of Jamaica was modelled on that of England, with its two Legislatures, and a system of administration entirely independent of the control of the Home Government. In one of his early despatches Mr. Eyre himself calls the attention of the Colonial Office to the utter inadequacy of the popular representation in the House of Assembly. He found that, since emancipation, the population had largely increased; that the education given by the various religious bodies had created a large number of intelligent coloured men who should have enjoyed a place in the administration of affairs. They had acquired property in land and in commerce, but were denied the franchise; so that the representative body consisted almost entirely of planters or their nominees, among whom the traditions of the time of bondage still held full sway. Thus, at the election of 1864, Mr. Eyre remarks that the number of persons qualified to vote for the forty-seven members of the House of Assembly was only 1,903. The actual voters were not more than 1,457, out of a population of 436,807 persons. He naively adds: "And yet Jamaica is said to possess representative institutions."

With rare exceptions the members chosen were all white men. It was the rarest thing in Jamaica to find a black or brown man on the benches of the Assembly. Yet the white population numbered only one to thirty-two black. No wonder that in response to Mr. Eyre's despatch, the Duke of Newcastle should declare, almost in the language of his predecessor Earl Grey, that, "while Her Majesty's Government are most

1*

desirous to exercise no unnecessary interference with the action of the Colonial Legislature, they are bound to bear in mind that the bulk of the population of Jamaica are not represented in its Assembly."

Such interference as the circumstances allowed was, nevertheless, constantly taking place. The approval of the Home authorities was frequently refused to laws of the most oppressive character. Of forty Acts actually passed by the Assembly in 1861-62, and allowed by the Colonial Office, only one in the slightest degree touched the well-being of the labouring classes—an Act about Industrial Schools. All the rest related to increased taxation, the increase of paid offices, Immigration Bills, which in no respect could be said to be beneficial to the labouring classes, and the like. Not one gave direct attention to the wants of the coloured people. Some were actually injurious to their welfare. The planters and the white population were careful of their own interests alone.

Mr. T. C. Burke, the member for St. David's parish, thus sketches, in 1865, the condition of the island, resulting from the course taken by the Jamaica Assembly, the members of which he did not hesitate to call "The Forty Thieves" :—

"Jamaica, he said, was pursuing a senseless struggle with the Colonial Minister, to the detriment of the best interests of the Colony. The result has been that no improvement has taken place in the moral or material condition of the bulk of the population, and they have been allowed to grow up in a state of semi-barbarism. Laws most injurious to their progress were passed, but which were, fortunately, disallowed in England. High import duties were imposed on the necessaries of life, thereby enhancing the prices, which necessitated the negro obtaining land for himself, and cultivating provisions, whereby the estates were deprived of labour. Everything was done to check the productive industry of the small settlers." "The result was," he added, "as Lord Grey wrote in 1852 :—' Although the need of well-considered legislation, to meet the wants of an entirely new state of society, was not less urgent in Jamaica than in the other former slave colonies; and though Jamaica has far greater facilities than most of these colonies for carrying into effect such measures as are required, the Statute Book of the island for the last six years presents nearly a blank, as regards laws calculated to improve the condition of the population, and to raise them in the scale of civilisation.'" *

It can create no surprise that, with a House of Assembly so constituted, there should rapidly arise causes of dissension between its members and the Executive Government. Early in 1864, the tension became so great that the House of Assembly resorted to the almost unprecedented step of forwarding direct to the Colonial Office a memorial to the Queen, in which it was stated, for reasons given, that the House had declined to do any further business with the Governor. They complain of his administration in many of its acts, and virtually pray for his removal.

---

* "Parliamentary Debates of Jamaica, 1865," p. 47.

Mr. Eyre immediately prorogued the **Assembly,** and chiefly on the ground that the resolutions adopted were passed by some thirteen out of forty-seven constituting the **House,** though after a very protracted debate, from which a large proportion of them were absent. On this account, Mr. Eyre was disposed to disregard the vote. But it would appear that the opinions of the absentees must have been in harmony with it; for on the reassembling of the House, on the 26th April, they allowed a somewhat similar **number** **to** reaffirm the vote, and to order measures to **be** taken for the publication of their resolutions in the **newspapers** of the island, and for their transmission **to certain named** members **of the** House of Commons, in order that their complaints might be heard in Parliament.

I do not think that this state of things can be laid entirely at the door of the Governor. There were doubtless faults on both sides. It was unfortunate; for these bitter disputes largely contributed to the distractions of the time, and destroyed every hope of good government. It was in vain for the Governor, in his speech to the Legislature in November, to appeal to them to "forget past differences," and to co-operate with him "to promote the common good." *

It might have been expected that when emancipation had become an unalterable fact, haste would have been made to bring the legislation of the island

---

* **Blue Book,** June 3rd, 1864, pp. 350 to 356.

into conformity with the new conditions; that some pains would have been taken to elevate the people, and to remove the multiplicity of evils which slavery had left as a malignant disease behind. On the contrary, an unreasoning and contumacious spirit took possession of Jamaica legislators. They rejected with heated words every proposal of the British Government which had in view the benefit of the negro. They exhibited at every turn an intention to coerce, as in the old time, their coloured fellow-subjects, and to make "their lives bitter with hard service." They threw every hindrance that could be imagined in the way of their enjoyment of their common rights. A small oligarchy of some 2,000 persons possessed themselves of the reins of administration, and laws of monstrous stringency were often passed, to limit unjustly, or to destroy, the freedom conferred by the mother country. The barbarities of a slave code were attempted to be perpetuated among a free people, and excessive penalties were inflicted on the slightest breach of intolerant laws. The expenses of the courts were made enormously heavy, so that, according to the report of a police magistrate, "the poor man was often debarred from seeking justice."

In view of subsequent events the following testimony of the Hon. Dr. Bowerbank, a member of the Island Privy Council, ought not to be withheld:— "After many years' residence here, and after sitting as a member of the House of Assembly for some three years, I feel bound in honour and in duty to express

my opinion that the House of Assembly is the curse
of Jamaica."

The futility of the legislation emanating from such
a body cannot be better stated than in the language
of Mr. Eyre himself; and it is the more important as
corroborating to the full the statements of my letter
to Mr. Cardwell, so often charged with exaggeration,
and even untruth. Writing to the Colonial Office on
the 2nd March, 1865, Mr. Eyre says :—" The young and
the strong of both sexes, those who are well able to
work, fill the gaols of the Colony. The commission
of crime and its consequences are little thought of,
and larcenies have increased to an alarming extent."
He then quotes, with approval, the words of a resident
on "the inveterate habits of idleness, and the low
state of moral and religious principles which prevail
in so fearful a degree in our community." Imprisonment and hard labour proved no check, and Mr. Eyre's
only remedy was a return to the lash, as a moralising
agency and deterrent of crime. "It is undeniable,"
he says, "that wages are lower and necessaries are
dearer than in former years ; therefore, the mere
labourer for hire is necessarily poorer. . . . Imported goods, especially clothing materials, have been
enhanced greatly in price since the commencement of
war in America. . . . Applications for private
relief are more numerous than formerly, and there
are, no doubt, many instances of extreme poverty and
distress, both in reference to food and as respects
clothing." He closes with the following emphatic
declaration, after his three years' government, of the

ruin which had fallen on Jamaica :—" Deterioration, decadence, and decay are everywhere noticeable, and the elements which ought to sustain and improve the national character, and promote the welfare and progress of the country, are gradually disappearing." *

This was Mr. Eyre's view of the condition of Jamaica at the very time that my letter came into his hands. At the same time all accounts concur in representing Mr. Eyre to have been, during the two years preceding the occurrences at Morant Bay, the most unpopular Governor who had held office in Jamaica for many years, and his unpopularity was not confined to the emancipated peasantry, it pervaded all classes of the population.

To complete this picture, I need only add the account given by Dr. Bowerbank of the influences at work which so injuriously affected the lower classes. He notes the acknowledged inefficiency of the courts of law; the failure of justice for the lower orders; the laxity, untrustworthiness, and improprieties of public boards; the gross and unblushing bribery and corruption practised at elections by the upper classes; the licentiousness and gross perversions of the truth, and the "immoral relations of the public Press"; the scandalous abuses, want of integrity and shortcomings,

---

° Blue Book on Affairs of Jamaica, No. 9, p. 7. For a full discussion of the subjects of the above paragraphs, see the searching inquiry of Mr. J. M. Ludlow, Barrister-at-Law, in his calm and judicial paper, entitled "A Quarter of a Century of Jamaica Legislation." Published by the Jamaica Committee, 1866.

in the management of public institutions ; the laxity, the perjury, the defalcations, and the frauds committed under the shelter of the laws ; the disgraceful bickerings and jobbery of the members of the Assembly. He adds to all this the scathing remark : —"It is unreasonable to expect that so imitative and cunning a class of men as the lower orders of this community, will see their betters in their own way set at defiance all law, and justice, and religion to obtain their own ends ; and that they will not in *their* own way follow the example set them to serve their own purposes." *

Bad as all this was, intensity was added to the discontent and disquietude existing among all classes by the severity of the drought which for three successive years had dried up the productive industries of agriculture. Through the failure of sugar cultivation, and the closing of more than one half the estates,† employment was steadily diminishing, and no persistent attempts were made to encourage the cultivation of minor products, such as coffee, cotton, ginger and other spices, arrowroot, &c., &c., while at the same time further taxation was laid on the necessaries of life. So far back as 1862 the Governor, in his speech to the Legislature, noted " the depreciation of the value of produce," and " the loss of con-

---

° Jamaica Blue Book, p. 78.

† Mr. Hosack, a member of the Privy Council, stated in May, 1865, that " there are about 300 sugar estates in Jamaica now remaining out of 700 once under cultivation."—Blue Book on Jamaica Affairs, p. 248.

siderable number of stock from drought." He also
refers to " the depressed circumstances of the Colony,"
and to " the unremunerative prices of produce." And
among his later despatches in 1865 (August 21st), he
reports that the colonists have " suffered very severely
of late years from the continual low prices and from
bad seasons." * The laws enacted in the Session of
1864 also bear testimony to the distress as giving
rise to more numerous offences calling for extreme
severity as the true remedy, and for which, in some
cases, only compulsory service would suffice.† In
the time of drought, heartless land agents were even
found who wantonly destroyed the produce of the
provision grounds, to the amount of £15 or £20,
arising from disputes about the ownership of rocky
lands in the mountains, which with immense toil the
negro agriculturist had brought under cultivation. ‡

---

* Blue Book on Jamaica Affairs, p. 251.

† See " Facts and Documents," p. 7. Published by the
Jamaica Committee.

‡ *Jamaica Guardian* of March 2nd, 1865.

CHAPTER II.

SUCH was the general state of the island at the time that my letter reached Mr. Eyre, at the end of the month of February, 1865. Mr. Eyre's relations with the House of Assembly, and with some members of the administration, were in a very strained condition. In a despatch, dated the 8th July, to the Colonial Office, he informs Mr. Cardwell that, although he had succeeded in passing some essential measures, and in obtaining the revenue necessary for the year, he had not enjoyed the co-operation of the Legislature in his efforts for the promotion of the public good. Still he hoped that much of the existing agitation would subside before the Legislature would again meet.*

My letter is first heard of, in the possession of the Hon. William Hosack, a member of the Executive Committee, and also a member of the House of Assembly, on the 28th February. It was in the hands of the Bishop of Kingston three days later, for, on the 2nd March, the Bishop had prepared a Circular of

---

* Blue Book on the Affairs of Jamaica, No. 5, February 8th, 1865.

Questions, addressed to a few selected clergymen, requesting replies by the 8th March. His Excellency the Governor was left at perfect liberty by Mr. Cardwell to seek information in any quarter that he might choose. For reasons unknown, the scope of his inquiries was almost immediately enlarged; for on the 13th March, a Circular was sent out, through official channels, to the custodes of parishes, the judges and magistrates, and subsequently to all the clergy and to ministers of religion of all denominations. It consisted of the despatch of Mr. Secretary Cardwell, with my letter, and requested these gentlemen to furnish the Governor with the materials for his reply. On the 21st March, a copy of the Circular was for the first time published in the *Jamaica Guardian*, by whose direction does not appear, but we are assured without Mr. Eyre's sanction or knowledge. The Circular issued by the Baptist Missionary Society in England, on the distress of the people of Jamaica, and calling for subscriptions, had already attracted the attention of the island press, but my letter, now printed, and its circulation by local authority, gave to the subject unexpected importance. It was not only placed in the hands of the leading officials and gentlemen of influence throughout the island, but was scattered broadcast, and it became at once the topic of heated discussion in every class of the community. It was reprinted in all the newspapers, and was the subject of daily comment. Not a house, not an individual, but was made acquainted with its contents, it was common property. The field labourer equally with the planter had it before him. It touched the welfare of rich and poor alike, and all without exception became intensely interested in its contents. Never was any official document printed and circulated which awakened such universal attention. Since the date of emancipation no subject had so seriously agitated the public opinion of Jamaica, or called forth more acrimonious discussion.*

In 1864, during the session of the Legislature, a few public meetings had been held to protest against the increased taxation proposed. It was said that already, under Mr. Eyre's administration, £300,000 had been added to the burdens of an impoverished people, much of which was spent, not for the public benefit, but for the profit of private individuals.

But popular feeling now found stronger and more definite expression in a series of public gatherings, which universally obtained the designation of "Underhill Meetings." The first was held in Savanna-la-Mar.† It was called on a requisition to the Custos of the parish, and was held in a schoolroom, the Courthouse being under repair. The chairman was a local celebrity, by name John Deleon, Esq. About 500 persons were present, and three or four magistrates. The purpose of the meeting was stated to be "the consideration of certain statements contained in a letter from Dr. Underhill, Secretary of the Baptist Missionary Society in London, to the Right Hon.

---

* Rev. D. J. East's "Reminiscences."

† "Parliamentary Debates," vol. xii., pp. 157, 183, 187, and 284.

Edward Cardwell, Her Majesty's Principal Secretary of State for the Colonies, in relation to the distress prevailing amongst the labouring population of the island." Four resolutions were unanimously passed. By the first it was affirmed that the peasantry, with all other classes of the community, "were severely suffering from the diminution of wages, consequent on the low value of the staple products of the country." The second resolution traces the depression to "the abandonment of so many of the estates," and the insufficiency of remunerative employment. The third resolution gave emphasis to the fact that no attempt had been made by the Legislature to relieve the distress, or to ameliorate the condition of the suffering classes. The final resolution directs that the proceedings of the meeting should be forwarded to the Colonial Office through the Governor, and be published in the newspapers, with the added suggestion that an impartial and effective investigation should be made by the Home Government.

The resolutions of the Montego Bay meeting took a somewhat wider scope. It was called by advertisement, and the Hon. G. H. Phillips, Custos of St. James, and member of the Privy Council, took the chair. All the resolutions were carried with perfect unanimity. The first resolution affirms that "distress pervades every section of the community, and the country is fast lapsing into ruin." It traces this state of things—(1) to the fiscal policy of the mother country, "which internal legislation and local rule have consummated," and they appeal to the Home

Government as alone capable of extricating them from their difficulties. (2) They declare that the evils they suffer are beyond their power to cure. The Legislature is unsuited to the country, its framework cumbrous and expensive, its corruption and extravagance unbounded, and they have no power to secure reform. The narrowness of the franchise throws all power into the hands of a few hangers-on in the capital, and neutralises the votes of the agricultural and commercial districts, while there exists in the Legislative Council and the Executive Committee no available check to the corruption and profligacy of the governing class. The resolutions close by saying that, "in review of the assertions made by Dr. Underhill, the meeting deliberately and unhesitatingly endorses their substantial truth." *

Another meeting of considerable importance—and which cannot be passed over—was held on the 3rd May in the city of Kingston. It was called in pursuance of a numerously signed requisition to the Hon. Edward Jordan, C.B., Mayor, who, at the last moment, on account of sickness, was unable to take the chair.† Mr. George William Gordon was therefore unanimously requested to preside. Mr. Wm. Kelly Smith, connected with the *Watchman* newspaper, was elected secretary. The *Jamaica Guardian* tells us that this was a large gathering of the so-called labouring classes, and the meeting was conducted in a

---

* Blue Book, " Papers Relative to the Affairs of Jamaica," p. 211.

† Report of Commission, p. 554.

regular and orderly manner. There were, however, some foolish statements made, which should be regarded as mere rhetorical flourishes, having no definite meaning in the speaker's own mind. After a few brief observations from the chair, on what the meeting was intended to be, fifteen resolutions were passed, and in a sixteenth, twenty gentlemen, mostly consisting of the proposers of the resolutions, were nominated to lay them before His Excellency the Governor, and to forward through him a copy to the Colonial Office. They deal with the same topics as the resolutions already given ; but are notable for the Christian spirit which pervades them. They affirm the truthfulness of Dr. Underhill's statements. The letter was a " gracious " interference, and a stimulus to the expression " of their distress, and of the wrongs and disabilities springing out of class legislation and mal-administration, which it was their interest and duty to endeavour to overcome in every constitutional way possible." They enter into some details of the injustice inflicted upon them by various parties, the low rate of wages and its consequences, the neglect of their representatives, the admission of immigrants, denial of education to the masses, taxation for the support of religion, and express their indebtedness to the philanthropic labours of their friends in England. They give their hearty thanks to Dr. Underhill and the Baptist missionaries, and express their belief that the course pursued by these gentlemen "is calculated to secure the best interests of all classes in the island."

2

Their final resolution is as follows :—" That, in keeping with the foregoing resolutions, this meeting calls upon all the descendants of Africa, in every parish throughout the island, to form themselves into societies, and hold public meetings, and co-operate for the purpose of setting forth their grievances, especially now, when our philanthropic friends in England are leading the way." *

The meeting did not attract much attention in Kingston at the time, but the parties who thus temperately set forth their grievances, and openly pursued a remedy for them in a legal and entirely constitutional way, are spoken of in the Governor's despatch to Mr. Cardwell as " political demagogues ready to stir up the people to a belief of imaginary wrongs," and not truly representative of the really thriving black and coloured population.

A reporter present thus gives the substance of the speeches he heard :—The people were sinking under the heavy burden of taxation. It was time to seek their liberties, for the black and coloured population were oppressed and kept under. Situations were not opened to them in the administration of affairs. The Government gave them no encouragement, although they were large taxpayers and were the larger section of the community. They had no advantages whatever, and it was only their duty to stand up as men and seek to enjoy their rights and privileges.

These statements were received with applause,

---

* " Papers Relative to the Affairs of Jamaica," pp. 189, 191.

especially when the people were assured that the Government was immoral and not to be obeyed. The Governor's morality proclamation, they said, was all a farce. This was true, for shortly after its issue appointments were made by Mr. Eyre of men of the very character which the proclamation denounced.

The resolutions were published, but the speeches were suppressed.[*]

Of the eleven meetings, of which records exist, not one was of more value and importance than that held on the 16th May in Spanish Town, at the seat of Government, called by the Hon. Richard Hill, a magistrate of eminent character and great influence. It was presided over by H. Lewis, Esq., one of the representatives of the parish in the House of Assembly. I shall venture to give these resolutions at length, inasmuch as they were personally presented by an influential deputation, specially named, to lay them before the Governor for transmission to the Colonial Office. A copy, over the signatures of the chairman and secretary, was also sent to me. They were unanimously adopted by the crowded assemblage :—

Resolved—

1. "That this meeting deeply deplores the present depressed state of the inhabitants of this Colony, and takes this opportunity of expressing its sentiments, especially at this period, when the philanthropists of England are trying to alleviate those distresses by bringing the same before the British Government."

---

[*] Royal Commission : The Evidence of George Fouché, p. 553.

2*

2. "That this meeting views with alarm the distressed condition of nearly all classes of the people of this Colony from the want of employment, in consequence of the abandonment of a large number of estates, and the staple of the country being no longer remunerative, caused by being brought into unequal competition with slave-grown products."

3. "That this meeting feels seriously the distressed state of the mechanics of this country, who are suffering from the injustice done to them, by the Legislature having imposed the same import duty of 12½ per cent. on the raw materials as on the manufactured articles imported into this island, not only from the mother country, but also from the United States, thus paralysing the industry and crippling the energies of the tradespeople of this country."

4 "That, in consequence of such distress, from no work being obtainable, many of the inhabitants, chiefly tradespeople, have been compelled to leave their homes to seek employment in foreign climes, and many others are only deterred from doing so, because they do not know what is to become of their families in their absence."

5. "That, as an illustration of the general distress, this meeting gives as an example that there are in Spanish Town, the capital of the island, nearly 150 carpenters, 60 masons, 91 shoemakers, 127 tailors, 772 seamstresses, and 800 servants, amounting in all to about 1,900 individuals, out of an adult population of 3,124 of all classes, many of whom are without knowing where to obtain their daily bread, and all of

whom are suffering more or less from the high prices of food and raiment, and excessive taxation."

6. "That, whilst recent legislation has been directed to endeavour to reduce crime by increasing the severity of punishment, no attention whatever has been given by the Legislature to the establishment of proper reformation, and a sound system of education."

7. "That, in reference to the letter of Dr. Underhill, addressed to the Secretary of State for the Colonies, we, Her Most Gracious Majesty's loyal subjects, assembled this day, do corroborate the statements made by that gentleman, and do most cordially record our grateful thanks to him for the warm sympathy he has evinced towards suffering humanity in this island."

8. "That a copy of the resolutions of this meeting be respectfully presented by a deputation appointed by the Chairman to his Excellency the Governor, to be by him transmitted to the Right Honourable Edward Cardwell, Secretary of State for the Colonies, and that a copy be forwarded to Dr. Underhill, and that the same be signed by the Chairman and Secretary on behalf of this meeting."

> *(Signed)*   A. H. LEWIS, Chairman.
>   JNO. S. M'PHERSON, Secretary.

Mr. Eyre has stated that "these public meetings were got up in many parishes, mostly through the agency of Baptist ministers, or others acting or professing to act in connection with them; and that Baptist

ministers, in many instances, took a prominent part
at such meetings, addressing the mob, and joining in
resolutions, adopting entirely, and vouching for, the
correctness of Dr. Underhill's allegations."

It was notorious that in no sense could these
meetings be called "a mob." If enthusiastic and
unanimous, they were in no instance disorderly.
Baptist ministers had in fact a very small share, either
in calling the meetings or in speaking at them. In
the parish of Trelawney, in which there were seven
Baptist ministers, with nearly 4,000 members, no
meeting whatever was convened, except a small one
by a pastor with his own church. In St. Ann's, in
which there were six Baptist ministers and upwards
of 3,500 church members, a public meeting was convened by the Custos; but the missionaries unanimously declined to take part in it. They were not
consulted and did not sign the requisition for it. At
Lucea the pastor was absent in England. The
Montego Bay meeting was the result of a parish
requisition numerously signed by all classes. It was
addressed by a member of the House of Assembly,
who read a letter from two estimable and wealthy
planters approving of the object of the gathering.*

It is certain that out of the twenty-one parishes in
which Baptist ministers laboured, the meetings were
held only in eleven. Of thirty-six recognised Baptist
ministers in the island, only seven European and four
coloured men took part. Of other clergymen and

---

* *Missionary Herald*, January, 1866, p. 13.

ministers who did address them, three belonged to the Church of England, two were Wesleyans, three were Presbyterians, and one was a Secession Methodist. In fact the meetings and their leaders consisted of thoroughly representative men, drawn from all classes, called out by the action, prudent or otherwise, of the Governor himself and his advisers.

The resolutions of the Spanish Town meeting are no more than a fair and unexaggerated specimen of the utterances of this popular movement. The meetings were everywhere largely attended, and the resolutions were enthusiastically carried. Such opportunities had never before been afforded for the expression of public sentiment on the part of the Freedmen and their descendants, or for the setting forth of the grievances under which they groaned. It was no part of Mr. Eyre's plans or intentions to awaken this somewhat dormant feeling. He had taken no pains to understand the real condition of the island, as seen from the point of view of the former serfs, of the white and propertied classes of the Colony. An opportunity had now come for the despised negro to give utterance to his complaints. The oppressed and down-trodden people were not without able expounders of their rights, men risen from their own ranks, who had happily enjoyed, and learnt to know the value of, the privileges which education, civilisation, and religion had brought to them at the cost, and by the instruction, of the Christian teachers in their midst. These men had been taught in the elementary schools of the missionaries, not of the State; for the time had not come for the Government to take the charge of their education. Reading and writing were their familiar acquisition. The Bible had been their Primer, and its Divine teachings familiarised them with the great law of righteousness—that law which exalteth a nation. Some of them had proved apt scholars.

Notably such men as Samuel Holt and Samuel Clark were able public speakers, and could express themselves in forcible Saxon speech. They were converted men and earnest Christian disciples. The very diction of the sacred volume had become to them their mother tongue. They were leaders among their brethren, loyal to the Queen, lovers of law and order, peaceable and peace-loving. But they were fully capable of appreciating their civil rights, and of standing before any audience to advocate and defend them. They knew their grievances, and could boldly claim relief from the burdens that class legislation unjustly imposed upon them. Holt attended and addressed several meetings on the north side of the island, always in the loyal and temperate spirit that characterised him, yet with a force and eloquence which facts within his personal knowledge naturally inspired.

As the " Underhill Meetings " proceeded, during the months of May and June, the excitement grew more intense, when a circumstance took place which added fuel to the flame. In the month of April, " An Humble Petition of the poor people of Jamaica and parish of St. Ann's," (so ran the title) addressed to the Queen, was forwarded to the Colonial Office by the

Governor.* In plain but forcible language it described the distress and grievances under which they were suffering. Mr. Eyre himself tells us that the petition represented " the peasantry of Jamaica as being generally in a destitute and starving condition." He does not deny the fact, but informs Her Majesty's Home Government that it was a statement which many of them " will be quite ready to take advantage of, and try to turn to their own account in every way they can." He feared that " these deluded people " would be led to expect relief, perhaps by pecuniary gifts, or by the removal of taxation, which they affirmed was unjust and oppressive.

The petition is expressed in language of childlike simplicity. It is warmly and affectionately loyal, a fair example of what the Secretary of the Royal Commission later on had in view, when he spoke of the negroes of Jamaica as " venerating the Queen with an almost more than English reverence." It describes for the Queen's information their daily life, the decayed state of the plantations, the difficulty of finding work and its poor remuneration ; that the little holdings and gardens some of them possessed were trampled under foot by the cattle of estate owners, who refused to repair the fences their cattle had broken down, or to compensate the loss. " If," say these trusting children, " our Most Gracious Sovereign Lady will be so kind as to get a quantity of land, we will put our hearts and hands to work and

* See Blue Book on Jamaica Affairs, pp. 235 and 241.

cultivate cotton, coffee, corn, canes, and tobacco, and other produce. . . . We are far away from our Gracious Queen, otherwise your humble servants would all speak to our Sovereign personally of our distress. . . . We the undersigned, your humble servants, have heavy taxes to pay, and have to pay the export duty on our little produce when selling it to the merchants. Your humble servants beg the notice of our Gracious Lady Queen Victoria, wishing her long life to reign over your poor and humble servants of the parish of St. Ann's." Of the 108 names appended to the petition only twenty-six could write, the rest affix a cross to mark their assent to the terms of the petition.

The reply reached them from the Colonial Office on the 14th June. In official and curt language these "humble" people are told that, as the means of support for the labouring classes depend upon labour, it is their duty, by industry and prudence, to use the means of prospering already in their hands, and to look to this source for their well-being, and not to rely on any schemes that may have been suggested to them. " Her Majesty will regard with interest and satisfaction their advancement through their own merits and efforts." *

It is difficult to believe that this document emanated from the home advisers of the Crown. It displays an utter want of sympathy and appreciation of the starving condition of the people, whom three

---

* Blue Book on Jamaica Affairs, p. 235.

years of drought had pauperised. In the island it was openly said to be, in substance, if not in form, the production of "King's House," in Spanish Town. It was immediately published by the Governor as a placard, with the heading, "The Queen's Advice," and 50,000 copies were sent for distribution to the officers of Government, to be posted in prominent places throughout the island. Copies were also sent to the clergy and ministers of all denominations, to be read from their pulpits.

To the people the disappointment was gall and wormwood, and but for the good sense and prudence of many ministers of religion, who refused to read it to their hearers—or, if read, it was with such comments as were calculated to allay the irritation, which might even then have culminated in general disaster. In one instance the Custos reported to the Governor that, on the **Rev.** M. Smith, the curate of Sacovia, reading the placard in his place of worship after service, the congregation hooted him out of the church; and that many members of the Bethlehem Moravian congregation, at the collection, told the minister they had no more to give him.*

It was heard with consternation by the well-disposed and thoughtful, who at once perceived how noxious would be its effect.† It was in truth a challenge provocative of an outbreak, rather than a well-considered effort to allay excitement. It sorely aggravated the popular irritation. It was written in

---

* Blue Book on Affairs, p. 241.
† Rev. D. J. East's " Reminiscences."

the spirit of the language of Pharaoh's taskmasters
to the Israelites, " Ye are idle, ye are idle." " Get you
unto your burdens."

" This," said Mr. Eyre, with bitterness, " is the first
fruits of Dr. Underhill's letter." " I fear," he adds,
" that the results of Dr. Underhill's communications
will have a very prejudicial influence in unsettling
the minds of the peasantry."* Certain it is, that Mr.
Eyre was himself, to a still greater degree, the real
agitator. To his unwise action must be attributed
the lamentable results which so speedily ensued. Mr.
Eyre, it must be supposed, was of the opinion of the
grand jurors of St. Ann's, that the petition might be
treated with scorn—as foolish tattle—since, as they
affirmed, the document was merely the " concoction
of some idle persons living about the villages," not
" vouched for " by their ministers " or any persons
of respectability."

No wonder that Mr. Eyre's already acquired unpopularity was deepened by this unfortunate event.
People longed for a change. Weak, vacillating, and
undignified in conduct and character, he proved himself to be a ruler lacking in tact, wisdom, and pene-
tration. His removal was regarded as an event to be
ardently desired, in order that the affairs of so fine
and important an island as Jamaica might be placed
in more capable hands. A leading paper, by no
means unfavourable to the Governor, describes the
Government House as neglected, so that even the

---

* Blue Book on Jamaica Affairs, p. 235.

ruling class was wearied with his ineptitude. Politically his government was a failure. It commanded no respect. It enjoyed neither confidence nor affection.* It was ever more ready to fall back upon barbarous means of punishment than to educate the people ; and to visit crimes with the whip, the crank, and the treadmill, which both the pulpit and press affirmed were the result of poverty and starvation, rather than of turpitude of heart.

° *Morning Journal* of July 8th, 1865.

CHAPTER III.

IF the loyalty of the people remained unshaken by the harsh and cruel indifference shown by Mr. Eyre and his advisers to the wretchedness and grievances pressing on their notice, from all parts of the island, the Governor at length began to fear that the agitation would take a violent direction and break out in open rebellion. The first indication of this expectation occurs in a despatch from Mr. Eyre to the Colonial Office, dated the 24th July. It is reported, he says, that a Mr. Hudson, writing on the 20th to the Hon. John Salmon, the Custos and President of the Privy Council, from the north side of the island, tells him that for the past few weeks there have been rumours of a rebellion among the peasantry, " to break out on or about the 1st August ; " that, in fact, " an organised plot existed having this as its end." He gives as his authority a house-girl in his family, who, if she knows more, refuses, he says, to tell it. He also informs the Custos that other persons (without naming them) had given intelligence of a like import. Two days later, the Custos adds the further information that he had been spoken to by several of the peasantry and coloured people about it; "but that I cannot arrive at any certain information." He further expresses the opinion that "it is unlikely, almost impossible, that the constantly referring to over-taxation and under-pay for labour, and unjust import duties, and unequal administration of the law, and impediments to export, and extortion and frauds—can do no other than create dissatisfaction among even the quietly disposed, and entirely prevent any good feeling growing up.* He, therefore, intimates that the presence on the coast of a vessel of war, with its morning and evening gun, would have a salutary effect, and check the evil intention if it really existed.

The day following the Custos of St. Elizabeth's mentions other rumours that had reached his ears; but he appears to have taken no steps to verify their truth. It sufficed, however, to determine Mr. Eyre to take action; for, on the same day, he writes to the Commodore of the Navy, giving him directions to send a man-of-war to the spot whence the rumours came. He is to visit the ports of Lucea, Savana-la-Mar, Montego Bay, and the mouth of the Black River, in the parishes of St. Elizabeth and St. James, all places on the north side of the island, where the agitation was reported to exist, stimulated by a few evil-minded persons. The Custos of the neighbouring parish of Westmoreland, however, writes Mr. Eyre on the 31st, that in his district he is not aware, nor does he think, "that there are any grounds, direct or

---

* Blue Book on Affairs of Jamaica, p. 248.

indirect, for supposing that any disaffection or intention to resist the law exists in any shape." * He
further takes the trouble to inquire into these
rumours, and reports that he could not find any pre-
parations being made for an outbreak ; that there was
no unusual demand for gunpowder or firearms. Still,
he would put the police on the watch. With regard
to the parish of St. James, he feared there was good
cause for apprehension.

A coloured gentleman, Mr. John Gilling, of Black
River, St. James, who had taken an active part in one
of "the Underhill meetings," writes, on the 1st August,
to Mr. Eyre with regard to complaints of a serious
nature made by the Custos against him, "That he was
the chief insurgent in the 'insurrection' which was
to take place on that day." † A more false and unfounded tissue of reports, he declares, "has never been
made up against his own and the unbounded loyalty
of the black population of the parish." As a loyal
subject he requests to be supplied with the information
given to His Excellency the Governor.

On the same day, the Custos of St. James himself
reports to Mr. Eyre, that he "cannot say that he has
seen or heard anything showing any combination
among the labouring classes for any acts of violence."
Five days later, he adds that he had not found it
necessary to take any precautions of the nature recom-
mended to him.

On the 3rd August, Captain Wake, commander of

---

* Blue Book, p. 248.   † *Ibid.*, p. 244.

H.M.S. *Bulldog*, who had been ordered to visit Black River, reports to the Commodore: "Hitherto everything has been perfectly quiet, and I see no reason to apprehend that it will be otherwise in future. The currency of mischievous reports among such an ignorant, thoughtless, and credulous people has not been without effect; but I cannot find out that there is any ground whatever for believing in a preconcerted rising of even that small portion of the population which is discontented."

In point of fact, it soon became clear that the rumours of revolt which disturbed the Governor, and led to his warlike and military precautions, and to the seizure in the post-office of the letters of the Baptist missionaries residing in that quarter of the island, had no foundation whatever. Undeniably there was great discontent and openly expressed dissatisfaction everywhere with the administration of affairs, fully justified by the bitter feuds that prevailed in the House of Assembly, and the miserable condition of poverty and nakedness of multitudes of the emancipated population; but there was no sufficient reason for the exaggerated fears of Mr. Eyre, nor any good cause to doubt the loyalty of the great body of the people.

It must, however, be noted that rumours of a disturbing character were not reported from St. Thomas-in-the-East, or from the south side of the island, of which Morant Bay was the centre.

3

CHAPTER IV.

IT was on the 15th May that the Colonial Office received the first batch of reports collected by Governor Eyre in response to the views expressed in my letter. They were eighty-eight in number. Others followed at various dates; the whole representing the views of the many different parties to whom the Governor had addressed his circular. The first two came from Mr. Hosack, a member of the Executive Committee, and from the Bishop of Kingston; followed by a long array of replies from the custodes of parishes, inspectors of prisons, and other Government officials, with special communications from clergymen and ministers of all denominations. These all were from the white portion of the community. The views of the black population came to Mr. Eyre unasked for, in resolutions from the "Underhill Meetings," and generally with an instruction that they should be forwarded to the Home authorities.

A long despatch accompanied these papers from the Governor himself,* passing them in review, with

---

* Papers Relating to the Affairs of Jamaica, presented to Parliament, February, 1866, p. 29, 139, &c.

his opinion as to their accuracy and value. The Report of the Baptist missionaries alone fills thirty-three folio pages in the Blue Book,* and consists of a series of replies to questions drawn up by the Council of the Baptist Union of Jamaica, representing seventy-three congregations, having 20,000 church members, and nearly 10,000 scholars in their day and Sunday schools, spread, with two exceptions, through every county or parish of the island. The Baptist congregations for the most part were composed of the labouring classes; and the missionaries, from their intimate relations and constant intercourse with them, were certainly amongst the best informed on their social circumstances and condition.

I may mention the chief subjects with which this important report deals, the details of which are clearly and accurately given both *in extenso* and in a tabulated form. The places are carefully described from which the information was drawn, and sorted under the following heads :—The first schedule relates to the poverty and distress prevailing in every district. Then follow the causes assigned for this state of things; the extent of the demand and supply of labour; the rate of wages generally prevailing; the prices of food and clothing; the agricultural employments of the people apart from the estates; the causes of the increase of crime, especially larceny; the taxation and the operation of the laws; and, lastly, certain topics specially relating to the larger towns.

---

* Papers Relating to the Affairs of Jamaica, presented to Parliament, February, 1866, pp. 139, 147.

It is not possible here to summarise the mass of fact and detail accumulated in this elaborate document, with its carefully drawn schedules and conclusions. A more searching investigation into the social and economic condition of a people was never undertaken. It is at once thorough and free from bias and from exaggeration of language. It abounds with irrefutable facts. Its moderation and candour, the care shown in the collection of facts, and in stating the conclusions to which the ascertained facts lead, commend it to every thoughtful reader, and give it authority on all the matters of which it treats. So far as I am aware, not one of its statements has been questioned by any person in a position to be conversant with the subject. It is even characterised by Mr. Eyre as a paper " very carefully and ably got up, and containing much interesting and valuable information." " As a whole, the report," he says, "is a very fair and candid one, and will convey to Her Majesty's Government much important and useful information." *

Yet with this document in his possession, Mr. Eyre, betraying a prejudice unsuited to his position, can write to Mr. Cardwell of "the serious mischief done amongst an ignorant and easily led population, when the missionaries residing amongst them, and professing to be their friends and instructors, endorse at public meetings—got up for the most part by political demagogues or designing agitators—such statements

* Blue Book : Papers Relative to Despatch, May 6th, 1865, pp. 139 and 140.

as those contained in Dr. Underhill's letter, to the effect that the population are driven to steal by starvation, and that the coloured population are denied political rights and just tribunals." * Many of the men thus censured had laboured in Jamaica with unimpeachable faithfulness for many years. To their efforts was mainly, if not solely, to be attributed the improvement that had taken place since emancipation in the social, moral, and religious character and position of the people. As men second to none in loyalty to the Crown, they were justified in regarding with indignation the uncharitable and undignified conduct exhibited by one holding Governor Eyre's high position as the representative of Her Majesty the Queen.

As might be expected, the resolutions emanating from the "Underhill Meetings" met with scant courtesy from Mr. Eyre. "They came," he frequently repeats, "from deluded people," from "political demagogues ready to stir up the people to a belief of imaginary wrongs"; "from an amalgamation (for political purposes) between a portion of the country party, who are opposed to the present Executive Committee, and a portion of the Baptist ministers who desire to back up Dr. Underhill." "Documents purporting to be a spontaneous emanation from the peasantry, but in reality got up by designing persons to serve their own purposes." † "Due entirely to Dr. Underhill's letter, and to the delusions which have

---

* Despatch of September 20th, 1865 : Papers relating to the Affairs of Jamaica, p. 262.

† Blue Book. Papers relative, &c., pp. 189, 197, 222, 226, 235.

been instilled into the minds of the ignorant peasantry
by designing persons in reference to it." Such was
the attitude of Governor Eyre to the vast mass of
coloured people who formed the bulk of the community. His bias was unmistakable, and his spirit
most lamentable.

The largest portion of these voluminous communications was in the possession of the Colonial Office by
the end of July. On the 5th August, Sir Frederick
Rogers, the Permanent Under-Secretary of State, informed me that a careful inquiry had been made into
the allegations of my letter, and " that the state of the
peasantry, as disclosed by that inquiry, is a matter
which has received, and will continue to receive, the
anxious attention of the Government of the Colony ;
but that it does not appear that they are suffering
from any general or continuous distress from which
they would not be at once relieved by settled industry." *

I was quite aware that the Home Government stood
in a very awkward and often strained relation to the
Colonial Executive in Jamaica. The so-called Representative House of Assembly enjoyed all the independent powers of the House of Commons. The Colonial
Office might suggest, but could not enforce. It might
give advice, but was powerless to secure its adoption,
Every attempt to bring the Jamaica Legislature
under the control of the Home authorities had been
baffled. Measures to secure the rights and the

---

* Blue Bock on Jamaica Affairs, p. 189.

improvement of the freed people of the island it had long been felt it was hopeless to expect. Class interests ever prevailed. The need of change, and a great one, had even forced itself on Mr. Eyre's consideration. "European proprietors," he said, "but above all European residents of position, education, and wealth, have dwindled down to an insignificant number; their places have not been taken by colonial-born persons of corresponding status and ability. Even now there is the greatest difficulty in adequately filling up the various offices in the State, such as the members of the Legislative Council, members of the House of Assembly, custodes of parishes, magistrates, departmental offices, &c. This state of things is getting worse year by year. The European element is continually decreasing, and my firm conviction is that the day will come, though it may yet be distant, when Jamaica will become little better than a second Haiti." *

But events were hastening on to a solution, for which it would seem the vilified letter of Dr. Underhill prepared the way.

Towards the end of August, the Colonial Secretary of State became aware of Mr. Eyre's apprehensions of "riots and rebellion among the peasantry in some of the parishes." My correspondents attached no importance to these rumours, except that one friend mentions that, to the surprise of everybody, "a man-of-war had come to Black River on that errand,

---

* Blue Book Despatch, August 19th, 1865, p. 247.

and that the captain with everybody else was woning where the treason could be, for they could not find it." No doubt, however, Mr. Eyre's tremors communicated themselves to the Colonial Office, and the excitement occasioned by Mr. Eyre's distribution of my letter was of a more serious and ominous character than they were willing to believe. If the authorities, both at home and in Jamaica, imagined that my statements, even if partially true, were mere exaggerations, there were certainly undeniable grievances enough to form a fitting nidus for the germination of any amount of discontent. Inflammable materials in abundance existed, only awaiting the accidental spark to burst into a flame. The Governor put the match to the tinder, and the publication of the placard, "The Queen's Advice," added to the already smoking heap.

From my intercourse with the Colonial Office, I had every reason to hope that the state of affairs would certainly obtain the best attention that could be given to it. From the known ability, wisdom, and skill of the Secretary of State I felt assured that every effort would be made to meet the crisis, and that measures beneficial to all classes of the population would be devised. I had perfect confidence in the goodwill of Mr. Cardwell, and that he would do all in his power to provide a remedy for the evils that were so threatening.

Writing Mr. Cardwell on the 17th August, I made the request that I should be permitted to peruse Governor Eyre's despatches, together with the replies to the inquiries he had set on foot, adding that I was given to understand that generally the facts to which I had called his attention were not denied, although opinion varied as to the causes of the distress. I also expressed the opinion that, unless measures of relief were speedily adopted, great disappointment would ensue, and the existing despondency of all classes would be aggravated, by the deceived expectations which the Circular of the Governor had awakened.

Sir Frederick Rogers replied, on the 30th September, that Mr. Cardwell would be pleased to permit me to peruse the documents received from the Governor of Jamaica and their voluminous enclosures, but as they were too numerous for copying, they were open to my inspection, at the Colonial Office, at any time convenient to me.* He adds:—" When you shall have read them, Mr. Cardwell will be glad to learn what specific action of the Government they appear to you to suggest, always bearing in mind that legislative action requires the concurrence and co-operation of the Legislative Council and Assembly of Jamaica." I was further informed that Governor Eyre did not attach much credit to "the rumour of riot and insurrection, expected to break out in consequence of delusions created in the minds of the peasantry, by designing persons taking advantage of the representations of hardships to which they are subjected."

I made immediate arrangements to avail myself of this permission, and, by the 9th October, I was ready

---

* Blue Book Papers, &c., p. 274.

to report the result of my examination. It appeared to me that a mere criticism of these voluminous documents would be of little value. It would be in many cases only one opinion set over against another opinion ; that questions were involved which deserved closer investigation, and should receive a more authoritative and impartial judgment. I felt, therefore, that, under all the circumstances, the suggestion made in my original letter of the 5th January was the most useful course, and, in the result, more surely beneficial—viz., " a searching inquiry into the Legislature and government of the island since emancipation, its taxation, and its economical and its social condition. This a *Royal Commission* only could effect, while its appointment was perfectly within the legitimate action of Her Majesty's Government."

This step I ventured again to urge on the Home Government. It had been more than once the subject of conversation with Mr. Cardwell. Among other reasons, I urged :—

1. It would at once allay the ferment and quiet apprehension. Despondency would yield to the hope of escape from the present distress, and time be secured for maturing the measures suited to the need.

2. It must be taken as a fact that, with few exceptions, the entire island was in a declining state, and that all interests were suffering.

3. It was most necessary, in order to avoid mistakes in the future, that the causes of the present lamentable state of affairs should be thoroughly sifted and inquired into by competent and impartial men.

4. It was specially urged that the course of legislation since emancipation needed investigation; that I had gone carefully through the titles of the Acts of the Legislature allowed by Her Majesty's Government from 1857 to 1865, 221 in number, and not more than two had for their direct object the benefit of the labouring population. One was concerned with the formation of an industrial school, and the other made provision for vaccination.*

5. The revenue and expenditure of the island, the mode of raising the revenue, and the incidence of taxation on the staple products needed revision.

6. Inquiry was also wanted into the working and results of the immigration laws, and into the serious mortality said to prevail among the immigrants.

7. A Royal Commission, visiting the island with ample powers, would be preferable to a Parliamentary inquiry in England, as the important evidence of the small freeholders and the peasantry, as well as that of other interested parties, could be obtained on the spot, and the investigation be made more thorough and complete.

8. The conclusions thus reached would afford a

---

* "I have often turned in disgust," said an able legal gentleman, a member of the House of Assembly in 1863, " against the imperfect system that at present prevails. I have often left the Court with a sense of shame for my country; and I am pained to think that the Government should show indifference in this matter. We cannot long continue as we are, if we are to be a civilised people." (*Jamaica Guardian*, September 28th, 1866.)

suitable basis for Parliamentary action should Her
Majesty's Government deem it advisable.

9. Lastly, the strained relations of the Home
Government with the Local Legislature could be
removed, and Her Majesty's Government be placed
in a position more effectually to exercise the protection demanded for the classes whose condition and
interests had hitherto been disregarded.

In closing it was added, " That I believe the measure
will be beneficial to the whole island. And even if it
should not lead to any Parliamentary or legislative
action on the part of Her Majesty's Government, the
facts collected and the conclusions arrived at would
be of the greatest service in correcting errors, in guiding administration, in stimulating the influential portion of the Jamaica community to diligent effort to
improve the classes below them, and in teaching all
parties that the interest of any one class is best served
by the prosperity and well-being of all."

The words of Lord Grey, one of Mr. Cardwell's predecessors in the Colonial Office, were in my mind:—
" The House of Assembly have ever used their power
to spare their own friends, and to burden severely
those who were opposed to them. The affairs of the
Administration were distinguished by corruption
and jobbing, and they exhibited a total want of
judgment in the local authorities in adapting their
measures to the existing state of things."

In a word, the representative Government of Jamaica
had proved itself to be a total failure, and must be
entirely reformed.

CHAPTER V.

THE OUTBREAK.

I T was not till late in September that the agitated state of Jamaica began to attract public notice in England. The first indication I can trace came to me in a request from the editor of the *Daily News* to write two or three articles on the subject. This I did in three communications, which appeared in three successive numbers of the journal, towards the end of October; but they were scarcely sufficient to prepare the English people for the very alarming news which reached the Colonial Office on the 16th November. The startling information was contained in a despatch from Governor Eyre, dated the 20th October. * He stated that a most serious and alarming insurrection of the negro population, attended with great loss of life and destruction of property, had broken out. Not, however, on the north side of the island, whence the rumours which so excited Mr. Eyre had originally come, but at Morant Bay, in the south-east, in the parish of St. Thomas-in-the-East, whence it spread rapidly through the contiguous parishes.

* Papers relating to the Disturbances in Jamaica, presented to Parliament, February, 1866, p. 1.

Two days later, on the 18th, the news was published in a supplement to the *London* *Gazette*, and appeared simultaneously in the *Times* newspaper. The same mail brought me a brief account from three correspondents confirming the full and more complete statements of the despatch. It so happened that by previous arrangement I went down early in the morning of that day to the Colonial Office, to confer with Mr. Cardwell on the proposal contained in my letter of the 9th October. I did not then know of the despatch with its serious information, nor of the grave accusations brought against me by Mr. Eyre. I found the Secretary of State too busy with the outgoing mail to see me, and at his request I had an interview with the Under-Secretary instead. He was in a state of great agitation, entirely uncommunicative on the grave matters that had arisen, and I soon left him, wondering in my mind at the fruitlessness of my visit. Calling on a friend on my way home, he met me with the question, "Have you seen the *Times?*" "No." "Don't you know the news from Jamaica?" I told him of the general information of the outbreak which my letters contained. He then made me acquainted with the fact that Mr. Eyre had thrown the blame of this "wicked rebellion" on my shoulders, and had charged me as the author and a component part of the disturbances which had broken out. I had afterwards reason to know that the Government, on Mr. Eyre's allegations, had under consideration the propriety of my arrest, and within a few days I had offers from two detectives to undertake any service I might desire for my protection. Of this, however, there was no need, and my friendly relations with the Colonial Office remained undisturbed.

There were few persons in Great Britain to whom the tidings did not come with a shock of surprise—a surprise that deepened into bewilderment and horror—when the country was told that a " rebellion " of wide proportions had suddenly burst forth, like a destructive volcano, in the Island of Jamaica, the actors in which had planned nothing less than the slaughter of every white inhabitant and respectable brown person, the seizure of their properties, and the separation of the island from the British Crown.

The centre of the uprising was a small seaside town, known as Morant Bay, in the parish of St. Thomas-in-the-East, in the County of Surrey. There the rebels had begun their career of slaughter and plunder. The magistrates, clergy, and other gentlemen of position were said to have been murdered in cold blood, while peacefully engaged in the administration of justice. Their bodies had been mangled in ways only to be paralleled by the atrocities of the Sepoy Mutiny in India. The rebels were further reported to have spread themselves over the surrounding country, plundering and burning the estates, and slaughtering their masters; with religious rites and drunken orgies, praising God for their victory.

With the news of the rebellion came also the news of its suppression. It had been almost as suddenly extinguished as it had flamed forth, quenched with an outpour of blood more frightful than the massacre which was its cause. Governor Eyre affirmed that the most hideous atrocities had been perpetrated by the rebels. The curate of Bath had his tongue cut out while yet alive, and an attempt was made to flay him. One person, a black gentleman, because he was a friend of the white man, was ripped open and his entrails torn out. Another victim was roasted alive. Many others had their eyes extracted, their heads cleft open, and their brains scooped out. Some of the bodies of the dead were half burnt; others were horribly battered and mutilated. The women acted worse than the men, the only redeeming feature being that not a lady or a child was injured; spared, according to some, for worse horrors when their captors should be at leisure to indulge their brutal passions.

But if such barbarities were reported to be the crimes of the rebels, the course taken by the Government and its soldiery had its horrors too. Three days, says the Governor, sufficed to check the progress of the rebellion and to stop the plunder of the estates. Although not a single soldier was resisted, killed, or wounded, for thirty days the sword was unsheathed, and the work of retribution went on. Captain Luke describes his men as riding "like devils" to the carnage. All rebels who were captured, after a short trial, and as short a shrift, were shot or hung. Many whose participation in the outbreak was not proved, were shot down without resistance on every roadside. Says Colonel Hobbs, "I found a number of special constables, who had captured a number of prisoners from the rebel camp. Finding their guilt clear, and being unable either to take or to leave them, I had them all shot. The constables then hung them on trees, eleven in number. Their countenances were all diabolical, and they never flinched the very slightest."

These men had no trial, and the deed was followed by setting fire to the people's homesteads. The guilt-less were plunged with the guilty into one common ruin. It is the same "gallant" soldier who tells us that he tied Paul Bogle's "valet" to his stirrup, and with a pistol at the lad's ear forced from him the recognition of the leaders of the rebels, among an immense gang of prisoners waiting to be shot on the morrow. *

Another English colonel boasted of having forced his wretched prisoners to hang each other, and tells how he put up a prisoner at four hundred yards as a mark for his riflemen.†

One intrepid officer gleefully tells us how "we shot two prisoners and catted five or six." Then a little

---

* Yet Colonel Hobbs, until this occurrence, was regarded as a humane and Christian man. At first indeed he could not be induced to pursue the cruel and vindictive course which had been initiated during the personal presence of Governor Eyre on the spot. For his reticence he was bitterly reproached. He at last gave way, and did deeds which occasioned him the bitterest anguish, which ended in a voluntary death. On his way to England he leaped overboard and was drowned.

† A highly esteemed friend informed me that on a visit a few weeks afterwards to the Blue Mountains, the very spot on the hill-side was pointed out to him, where the poor fellow Welling-ton was set up as a target for the soldiers to fire at.

further on, how they flogged nine unarmed men. In a raid the next day, with thirty of his band, three negro homesteads were burnt; several black men were flogged without court martial; nine others were tried, one received a hundred lashes on the spot, and the rest were shot or hung. "Such," he coolly adds, "is martial law." "The soldiery enjoy it, the inhabitants have to dread it. If they run, they are shot for running away. The contents of all the houses have been reduced to a mass of broken and hacked furniture."

Of the Courts Martial I need not speak here at length. On the flimsiest evidence, or no legal evidence at all, hundreds were condemned to death, and with jocund shouts led to execution. The homes of the peasantry, for miles beyond the scene of the disturbances, were recklessly burnt and their contents destroyed. Women and children were sent adrift without clothing or food. Cruel scourgings, in some cases with piano wire twisted up with the cords, were freely inflicted. A scowling look was sufficient to bring down vengeance upon the wretched captives. Women were not exempt from torture and insult. And so the carnival of blood went on; the "fun" of the pastime "ran fast and furious."

Besides these terrible exploits on the area of the outbreak, arrests were made and threatened in other parts of the island; and the prisoners, in order to secure their conviction, were carried, against all law, into the districts where martial law was in force. In this way, Mr. George William Gordon, having surrendered in Kingston, was borne to Morant Bay, as

the chief instigator of the rebellion, because it was
certain that legal evidence could not be obtained
to secure his condemnation by the ordinary civil
tribunals. On the slightest pretext, he was found
guilty and led to execution. Others, even, if possible,
with less justification, without either judge or jury,
were cruelly tortured and then imprisoned. A reign
of terror was established, and no man's life was safe.
The most estimable and peaceably-minded men were
not free from suspicion of complicity with the rebels.
They scarcely dared to open their lips to their dearest
friends. Letters were intercepted in the post office,
to find matter of accusation against men of known
integrity and good social position. Said a resident
of the district, writing at the time :—

"We are living in fear all the day long. Our lives
were in danger during the first few days of the rioters'
success, and were not less so when they were crushed.
Martial law is a dreadful thing! a horrible affair!
The soldiers were let loose in the country, and did
their work with savage fury, shooting down good, bad,
and indifferent, spreading death and desolation. The
road for miles was said to have been insufferable, from
the stench of the rotting bodies of men and women." *

The outbreak was indeed awful in its massacre and
diabolical in its cruelty ; but it would be hard to find
words to express the terribleness of the retribution
with which it was visited. Although the Governor
himself went to the spot, he, it would appear, did not

---

* The *Freeman*, January 3rd, 1866.

attempt to exercise any restraining influence over
these shocking barbarities.

I have written this succinct narrative of the outbreak and its suppression, as it was given and
published for the information of the English people
by Governor Eyre and his subordinates, in order that
my readers may understand the exciting cause of the
remarkable agitation which ensued in this country, on
the "Rebellion" and the character of its suppression
becoming known.   It led the Home Government
immediately to resolve on the suspension of Mr. Eyre,
to the formation of a Royal Commission to make a full
inquiry into events so fraught with misery, cruelty,
and horror, and finally to Mr. Eyre's supersession and
removal from an office for which he had shown such
signal unfitness.

It is some alleviation to this terrible picture to
know, from the investigations of the Royal Commission,
that in a certain degree these accounts, rendered by
the local authorities, and by the actors in the tragedy,
were much exaggerated.   The reality was bad
enough, but the story came to this country darkly
coloured by the rage and revengeful feelings of the
men engaged in the suppression.   The number of
persons killed by the "rebels," as accurately ascertained by the Royal Commissioners, was in all twenty-
two, white and black ; but the horrible outrages on
the dead, so minutely detailed in the despatches, had
no existence.   On the other hand, the Commissioners
establish the fact that at least 430 persons were shot
or hung in retaliation during the existence of martial

law. They declare that the punishments inflicted were indeed excessive; that many sufferers were entirely innocent of any crime whatever; that a thousand dwellings were wantonly and cruelly burnt; and that certainly not fewer then six hundred persons were scourged in a most reckless manner, with the greatest barbarity, at Bath, with cats having piano wire inserted in the lash; while many, after flogging, were sentenced to various terms of imprisonment.*

With the full concurrence of all parties in the State, the Home Government resolved to send out without delay a Royal Commission armed with all necessary authority. The Commission was proclaimed under the Royal Sign Manual on the 30th December. Sir Henry Storks was placed at its head, as Captain-General and Governor-in-Chief of Jamaica and its dependencies, having as his colleagues on the Commission, Russell Gurney, Esq., Recorder of the City of London, and J. B. Maule, Esq., Recorder of Leeds, with C. S. Roundell, Esq., as Secretary. They were directed to "prosecute an inquiry into the nature and circumstances of certain disturbances which had occurred in the Island of Jamaica, and with respect to the measures adopted in the course of their suppression." The Commissioners met in Spanish Town, in Jamaica, on Saturday, the 20th January, and formally opened their inquiry on Tuesday, the 23rd. They began to receive evidence on the following Thursday. In the course of the

---

* Report of the Royal Commissioners.

investigation they recorded the evidence of 730 persons, and visited several times the scene of the outbreak.   By the 9th April their work was finished.

But before dealing with the Report of the Commission it will be necessary to give, in a little more detail, the series of events which preceded the outbreak, and the steps taken by the Jamaica authorities.

CHAPTER VI.

ORIGIN AND CAUSE OF THE OUTBREAK.

THE parish of St. Thomas-in-the-East was one of the many localities in which, from the abandonment of estates and other circumstances, some of which will presently appear, "employment on hire could not now be obtained by all the peasantry, even if disposed to labour." * And although Mr. Eyre had not received from this district any information that it was ripe for "rebellion," difficulties with regard to the ownership and tenure of land were fruitful of great discontent.

One of the last localities, in which an "Underhill Meeting" was held, was Morant Bay. It was called on Saturday, the 12th August, by the Custos of the parish, the Hon. Baron von Ketelhodt, on the requisition of a numerously signed memorial. At this meeting, Mr. G. W. Gordon, the representative of the parish in the House of Assembly, took the chair. A long string of resolutions was unanimously adopted, in which special attention was given to the misgovernment of the island, the increasing taxation,

---

* Blue Book relative to the Affairs of Jamaica : Eyre's Despatch, September 20th, 1865, p. 262.

the depressing effects of the low rate of wages, with the irregularity of their payment, the miserable condition of the people with regard to clothing and other necessaries, the enactment of oppressive laws, more especially complaining of the arbitrary, illegal, and inconsistent conduct of the Custos, as destructive of the peace and prosperity of the parish.*

It was unfortunate that Mr. Gordon, though from his public position entitled to the honour, was called to the chair, seeing that a long-standing feud existed between him and the Custos, who, after summoning the meeting, attempted to prevent its taking place. The local magistrates were notoriously corrupt ; and, owing to their one-sided, unjust, and selfish decisions, the labouring population had lost all faith in their judicial impartiality. So much was this the case, that they had ceased to bring their grievances to the Sessions Court, and sought the settlement of their disputes by secret and irregular tribunals of their own. Beyond this, there is no evidence of any intention to violate the laws of the land. Indeed, we have it on the assurance of Mr. Eyre, on the 4th November, after the outbreak had occurred and was put down, that there " was no organised or combined action." †

The good faith of the people is made clearly manifest by the fact, that they sent a deputation to Spanish Town to lay before His Excellency the resolutions of the meeting. They trudged the weary forty miles on

---

* From the placard containing these statements. It was sent me by direction of the meeting.

† Papers on Disturbances in Jamaica, Part I., p. 79.

foot to see him, that they might personally lay their grievances at his feet; but the Governor not only declined to listen to them, but refused to admit them to his presence. The rebuff sent them home with sore hearts, and the report of their treatment increased the bitter feeling existing. Their last hope was gone. He whom, as the Queen's representative, they rightly expected to be their friend, acted as their foe. Their leaders deeply felt the insult, and their enemies triumphed over their defeat.

For the proper understanding of what follows, it must be remembered that nothing had been done to improve the character of the local Courts, before which there had been many cases relative to the occupation of land in the district. The Royal Commissioners, in their report, explicitly state that "the difficulties in the way of seeking relief by law were very great, and it was not to be expected that, constituted as the bench of magistrates at present is, it would have the confidence of the labourers. The magistrates are principally planters and persons connected with the management of estates. Those who are not so connected are for the most part engaged in business, and their attendance is very irregular." Questions "are adjudicated upon by those whose interests and feelings are supposed to be hostile to the labourer and the occupier." *

The evidence is conclusive that the Petty Sessions Courts were presided over by partial judges; that the

---

* Papers on Disturbances in Jamaica, Part I., p. 79.

costs were extravagant, and that the sentences were
severe even to injustice upon the labouring class
and lenient upon the higher. A stipendiary magistrate declared that the prevalent dissatisfaction
was well grounded. He had in his possession, he
said, instances of direct acts of oppression. Two
gentlemen had gained an unenviable notoriety for
their oppressive and unjust conduct. One was the
Custos himself, the other was a clergyman of the
Church of England. They seem to have acquired
specially the hatred of the peasantry, and were among
the first victims in the "disturbances" that ensued.
The Church and the owners of sugar estates, were
believed to be confederates in their hostility to the
labourer.

The riot began at a Court of Petty Sessions held on
Saturday, the 7th of October. It was a market day,
and a large number of persons had collected for the
sale and purchase of their produce. The presiding
magistrate was the Custos, the Baron von Ketelhodt.
The business which came before the Court consisted
chiefly of charges of assault and the use of abusive
language. One was a case of assault brought by a
woman against a boy. He was convicted and fined
4s., with costs, amounting to 12s. 6d. When called
upon for the fine and costs, a man present in Court
told him to pay the fine only, and not the heavy costs
which were added to it. This caused so much disturbance that business was for a time suspended.
The magistrates ordered that the man by whom the
interruption was made should be brought before them.

The constables arrested him, but he was at once rescued by the bystanders. Followed by the police outside, he was again seized, and again rescued. The police were beaten, and compelled to release their prisoner. The numerous attendance of the people at the Court, on that day, was occasioned, however, by a more important matter. It arose out of a dispute as to the rightful possession of some land at a place called Stony Gut, a negro settlement about five miles from Morant Bay. It had been leased out, by whom does not appear; but the occupiers had refused the rent for their holdings, on the ground, it was said, that the land was free and the estate belonged to the Queen.

The case had been previously adjudicated upon by the Court; but during the summer it had again been a subject of dispute. On this occasion, it was for a trespass on a part of this estate that a man named Miller was summoned. It was decided against him by the planter magistrates; but notice of an appeal was given.*

On the following Monday, warrants were issued against two persons of the name of Bogle and several others, charged with having taken part in the riot of Saturday. Six policemen and two constables proceeded to Stony Gut on Tuesday morning to arrest the Bogles and their associates. Paul Bogle resisted his

---

* As the trespass complained of involved a question of title, it ought to have been tried by a judge and jury. The Petty Sessions Court seems to have had no rightful jurisdiction in the matter.

arrest, and was speedily assisted by some three to five
hundred men.   Armed with cutlasses, sticks, and
pikes, they rushed out from a chapel near at hand,
where they had assembled, and of which Bogle was
the preacher or leader.   The police were overpowered
and severely beaten, and three were, for a short time,
detained as prisoners.   In the evening information
reached the authorities at Morant Bay that the
rioters would, on the following day, Wednesday, the
11th October, appear at the Vestry then to be held,
to state anew their grievances.   The Custos, fearing
further disturbances, summoned the Volunteers of
the district, and also wrote to the Governor for
military aid.

That there was no formed intention on the part
of the people to rebel or resist the authorities is
clear from the fact that, on Monday, the 9th, some
twenty persons, including three Bogles, forwarded
a petition to Mr. Eyre, which must have been
received on the next day, as it was replied to by
the Governor on the 12th.   In this they complained
that an "outrageous assault" was made upon them
on Saturday, by the policemen of the parish, on the
order of the Justices; that warrants had been issued
against innocent persons which they were compelled
to resist; they therefore called upon His Excellency
for protection; that for twenty-seven years, though
always obedient to the Queen, they had " been imposed
upon," and could no longer endure it.   If refused,
they had no other alternative than to put their
"shoulders to the wheel."

The Governor's reply repeated, in his set phrase, that they were "misled by the representations of evil-disposed and designing men"; that he was ready to listen to their complaints, but not to any application accompanied by threats; and that it was His Excellency's determination to vindicate and uphold the majesty of the law.

It is obvious that, at this supreme moment, kind treatment and an effort to deal impartially with grievances, which unquestionably had just foundation, would have averted the calamity that fell on the magistrates and community of Morant Bay on this Wednesday afternoon. The Custos, magistrates, and vestrymen met at noon in the Court House, and the ordinary business was transacted; but it would appear that not the least effort was made to meet the prayer of Mr. Eyre's petitioners. Between three and four o'clock a crowd of people gathered about the Vestry Hall, some of them armed with cutlasses and sticks, and with other weapons which had been taken from the police station. They assembled in a large open space facing the Court House, in front of which the Volunteers had been drawn up. Their presence was provocative of anger, and the coming forward of the Custos was the signal for its expression. The attitude of the people became more threatening when the Custos began to read the Riot Act. Then, it is said, stones were thrown, one of which struck the captain of the Volunteers. The Custos, without further warning, gave the word to fire. The order was obeyed, and some of the people fell. It is a disputed point, however, whether the stones were thrown before the firing commenced ; but the Royal Commissioners conclude that they were most likely thrown by the women, and not by the main body of the people now advancing in mass towards the Volunteers. At the time of firing the insurgents were close upon the soldiers. The volley took effect, and infuriated them. There was instantly the cry of " War," and the rioters rushed forward. A few of the Volunteers were disarmed, the rest fled or took shelter in the Court House with the magistrates and the members of the Vestry. Some escaped by the back windows, others remained exposed to the now pelting shower of stones, and to the shots fired by the mob outside. Soon after the school-house was set on fire, which spread to the Court House, driving its inmates from the building. Favoured by the darkness, they concealed themselves in different places near at hand. "Some remained undiscovered, but others were dragged from their hiding places, and, one by one, either beaten to death or left for dead on the ground." *

That several meetings had been held in the neighbourhood, especially at Stony Gut, consequent on the refusal of Mr. Eyre and the authorities to remedy the grievances of the people, there can be no doubt. The reports of the proceedings that took place are, however, vague and contradictory, and it is altogether doubtful whether there existed any organised or combined

* Royal Commissioners' Report, p. 12.

action, beyond that which the bitter sense of common grievances, and deeply felt injuries of long duration, would produce. The result was most lamentable, and deserves the strongest condemnation. The number of persons killed by the rioters in and about the Court House appears to have been eighteen; the wounded amounted to thirty - one. Two of those most obnoxious, who fell, were the Custos and a clergyman, whose oppressive acts of injustice had specially roused the passions of the people.

The confusion spread like wild fire, and as the cry, "There is war at the Bay!" reached the mountains above Morant Bay, where the people were quietly working in the fields in utter ignorance of what was being done in the plains, the hoe and the machete were at once thrown aside, and they flew to the scene of conflict.* The only motive that actuated them was curiosity to see what was going on, and probably to share the spoil. In a few days the insurgents are said to have spread themselves over some thirty miles of country. Success led a few to entertain the wildest notions. Some hoped to become possessed of the estates which, in many instances, were carefully pre-served from plunder. A few imagined that the Government itself would fall into their hands. But after the first access of fury they ceased to kill their adversaries. The superior forces called forth by the Government, and the fearful retribution which fell upon

---

* This was stated to my informant by two young men, nephews of a mountain coffee-planter, who afterwards became Custos of the parish.

the rioters, speedily crushed any hope of success. In three days the rebellion was at an end, or, to use the words of Governor Eyre, " Our most important work being done, and the troops comfortably established in their barracks, we had for the first time a night of quiet and rest on the night of Sunday, the 15th October." * This was on the fourth day after the outbreak.

But the day of retribution had come. Martial law was proclaimed on Friday, the 13th, and at daybreak on Monday, the 16th, the first Court sat to try prisoners. Twenty-seven were found guilty and hung, Mr. Eyre having himself on the previous Friday visited Morant Bay to inaugurate the reign of terror that now set in. He returned to Kingston on the evening of the same day, but martial law remained in operation until the 13th November.

It is unnecessary that I should trace, step by step, and day by day, the atrocities that were perpetrated under the shield of martial law. It must suffice to give here in full the conclusions to which the Commissioners were led—the summing up of their investigation.†

1. " The continuance of martial law in its full force, to the extreme limit of its statutory operation, deprived the people, for a longer than necessary period, of the great constitutional privileges by which the security of life and property is provided for."

2. " The punishments inflicted were excessive."

---

* Despatch of 20th October, **p. 5.**
† **Report of the Commissioners, p. 41.**

3. "The punishment of death was unnecessarily frequent."

4. "The floggings were reckless, and at Bath positively barbarous."

5. "The burning of 1,000 houses was wanton and cruel."

The number of persons executed by the order of courts-martial was ascertained to have been 354; there were shot or hung or killed without trial, 85; a total of 439. Of these 147 were put to death after the 25th October, when all resistance and necessity for speedy punishment had entirely ceased. The Commissioners, moreover, distinctly state with regard to those brought before the courts-martial and suffered death, "There were many who were neither directly nor indirectly parties to the disturbances which it was the object of those in authority to suppress." The evidence given was "wholly insufficient to justify the findings."

I have already remarked that the statements of Governor Eyre as to the terrible mutilations and atrocities alleged to have been perpetrated by the black people on the whites were proved to have been unfounded. The persons murdered at Morant Bay were in various ways killed or beaten to death; but the brutalities and horrors, which reminded Mr. Eyre of the Sepoy Mutiny, were found to be purely imaginary, as were the vast numbers of plots and conspiracies which in their panic the Governor and his advisers fancied were thick about them. In the same way, the vauntings of the officers and others engaged in

5

the suppression, as to the numbers they had shot, hung, and flagellated, were found to be very inaccurate, and their pictures of the multitudes they had disposed of were discovered to be exaggerated. If the English people were horrified at their tales, and at the levity with which they were recorded, and resolved to have an inquiry, the Governor and his subordinates have themselves to thank for it, for they were the authors of the despatches and letters in which, with so much boastfulness and glee, they reported the magnitude of their exploits, and the " fun," and the slaughter, in which they had revelled. Still, allowing for their exaggerations, enough remains for the most emphatic condemnation and agonising grief.

It must not be forgotten that blood was first shed by the authorities on the spot. Frightful as was the revenge taken by the rioters on their oppressors, there is abundant proof that a spirit as malevolent and bloodthirsty actuated their white adversaries. The Royal Commissioners were constrained to endorse the public opinion of England and Europe, that the cruelties of the suppression were horrible and inexcusable.

CHAPTER VII.

THE island was beginning to recover from the state of panic into which it had been thrown by the Morant Bay outbreak, when the Legislature, at the call of His Excellency the Governor, met on the 7th November for the despatch of business. Though martial law was in operation for another six days, and arrests were continually being made, and sent before the courts-martial for trial, Mr. Eyre was able to inform the members of the two Houses that, what he called, "this most diabolical conspiracy to murder the white and coloured inhabitants of the Colony," had been "effectually subdued," and "the chief instigators of it" punished with death. He stated that this surprising feat had been accomplished "within three days of the first tidings reaching Kingston," and that the rebellion, by his "well-devised arrangements, had been headed, checked, and hemmed in ; and within a week fairly crushed."*

Certainly, if the origin of the rebellion was the result of a "wide and deeply-rooted conspiracy," the Governor might well congratulate himself and his

---

* "Parliamentary Debates of Jamaica," vol. xiii., p. 2.

5*

audience, not only on the rapidity and thoroughness
of its suppression, but that history does not record so
remarkable an instance of courage, energy, and
success. "All vied with each other," he said, "in
zealously doing their duty, and that they did it well
is evidenced by the successful results attained."

It was now an imperative duty to take the measures
which might avert in the future a recurrence of such
frightful events. "Those measures," said His Excellency, "may be summed up in a few words. Create a
strong government, and then, under a firm hand to
guide and direct, much may be accomplished. In
order to obtain a strong government there is but one
course open to you—that of abolishing the existing
Constitution (compensating the officers whose offices
are abolished), and establishing one better adapted to
the present state and requirements of the Colony. I in-
vite you then, Gentlemen, to make a great and generous
sacrifice for the sake of your country, and in immo-
lating on the altar of patriotism the two branches of
the Legislature, of which you yourselves are the con-
stituent parts, to hand down to posterity a noble
example of self-denial and heroism."

That a great change was absolutely necessary few
persons could be found to deny. The Home Government had long desired it. In 1839, and again in 1849,
the Parliament of Great Britain had been asked to
sanction some such course, but without success.
Governor Barkley, in 1854, had succeeded in intro-
ducing a small executive body, or cabinet, responsible
to the House of Assembly, but it brought about no

material improvement in the conduct of affairs. Even so late as July 7th, 1865, Mr. Cardwell had written to the Governor urging some such measure. He says, "With respect to the complaints of the conduct and constitution of the Legislature, if the majority of the Assembly could be induced to pass enactments in amendment of its own Constitution, Her Majesty's Government would be ready to give these enactments its most attentive and favourable consideration." *

In anticipation of a favourable occasion arising for the introduction of such a measure, an elaborate Bill had already been prepared, "for altering and amending the political Constitution of the island." The opportunity had now come. It was brought in and read a first time on the 9th November, on the second day after the meeting of the Assembly, and urgently pressed on the members for immediate adoption. Advantage was promptly taken of the existing terror to promote a measure which, in calmer times, would certainly have met with the most strenuous opposition. But Mr. Eyre had given so bright and cheering a view of the success of his military operations, that it became necessary for his purpose not to suffer the panic-feeling to subside.

It was nevertheless, he said, his "duty" to point out that the "entire Colony has long been, and is still, on the brink of a volcano which may at any moment burst into fury." Disloyalty, sedition, and murderous intentions were disseminated, and in some instances

---

* Papers relative to the Affairs of Jamaica, February, 1866, p. 205.

openly expressed in almost every district. The mis-
apprehensions and misrepresentations of pseudo-phil-
anthropists in England and Jamaica, inflammatory
harangues, and seditious writings of evil-minded men
of higher position, and of better education, and other
worthless persons, were very prevalent. To all this
must be added the personal, scurrilous, vindictive, and
disloyal writings of a licentious and unscrupulous
press. Even ministers of religion, "sadly so mis-
called," by their misguided counsels, have led to their
inevitable result in exciting to rebellion, arson,
murder.

Well might His Excellency say of his own statements, "These are hard and harsh words, Gentlemen,
but they are true, and this is no time to indulge in
selected sentences or polished phraseology. A mighty
danger threatens the land—we must examine boldly,
deeply, and unflinchingly, into the causes which have
led to this danger."

And yet, as if frightened by his own dark forebodings, Mr. Eyre immediately adds, "I know of no
general grievance or wrong under which the negroes
of this Colony labour. Individual cases of hardship,
or injustice, must arise in every community; but as a
whole the peasantry of Jamaica have nothing to complain of." Still it was necessary to draw this terrible
picture of the condition of the country, in order to
convince or frighten the members of the Legislature,
"how widely spread, how deeply rooted, the spirit of
disaffection is; how daring and determined the intention has been, and still is, to make Jamaica a second

Haiti, and how imperative it is upon you, Gentlemen, to take such measures as, under God's blessing, may avert such a calamity."

But were these representations true? Ought not such language to have been supported by substantial evidence? For two hundred and fifty years Jamaica had possessed a representative Constitution; would it not be an eternal disgrace to the Colony to destroy its very existence, unless the statements of the Governor could be substantiated? "Evidence is what we want," said the Hon. H. A. Whitelock; "and for the sake of the island, for the sake of peace, and considering that other countries are looking on us with watchful eyes, we ought to seek for such evidence. . . . We have no evidence of our own; the Governor has furnished us with none." *

Again and again members of the Assembly urged investigation, and the production of proofs for the Governor's terrifying words. They were not forthcoming. It was replied that the evidence was confidential, and could not with safety to the parties who gave it be divulged. The danger was real and great; the dark, thunderous clouds were ready to burst and overwhelm the whole island in ruin, and time must not be wasted in prolonged inquiries. Were not the signs of another storm visible to every eye, and needed no corroboration?

Among the voluminous papers laid before Parliament, I have found but one official document that in

* "Parliamentary Debates of Jamaica," vol. xiii., pp. 31, 90, and 93.

any degree can be said to support Mr. Eyre's affirmations ; but even this was not laid before the Assembly, and was known only to the Legislative Council. It consists of an extract from a letter addressed to Governor Eyre, on the 23rd November, by Colonel Whitfield, on the result of a visit he had paid to the detachment of soldiers located in his district, on the north side of the Island. The Colonel says : " I think that a considerable amount of intercommunication has and is taking place between the disaffected in the different parishes, for I observe men of sullen and dissatisfied looks riding about the country in all directions. About one half of the negroes look happy and contented, the remainder as if they would take much pleasure in cutting our throats. I think the same feeling exists among the women. But I do not think this feeling is confined to the district between Savanna-la-Mar and Montego Bay, but everywhere." To such evidence as this may well be applied the language of a member of the House of Assembly. We ought " to probe the matter carefully, and see if the fears that have been expressed were entertained advisedly."

I may set over against this the testimony of my friend, the Rev. D. J. East, relating to the same district of the island : " A day or two after the Morant Bay riot I made a journey, accompanied by one of my daughters, from Rio Bueno to Lucea, passing through the greater part of Trelawney and the parishes of St. James and Hanover. On the way, being well known, I was repeatedly stopped by numbers of the peasantry, who thronged the roads on their way to their respective markets (it being Saturday) to answer inquiries as to the rumours they had heard of the disturbances. All through these parishes it was evident that so far from the people being in any way implicated in these occurrences, or with their perpetration, they were in utter ignorance. At Lucea, on the Sunday morning, I preached a sermon on 'Civil Government,' setting forth the obligations of subjects to their rulers. I delivered the same sermon at Montego Bay, both times to crowded audiences, who evinced the fullest sympathy with the teaching of the New Testament as expounded to them." *

It was soon apparent that the state of the island did not justify Mr. Eyre's strong and urgent representations. The measure of the Government was exceedingly distasteful to the majority of the House. Even the placemen and partisans of the Administration who occupied its benches and filled the offices of the State, although promised compensation should they sustain any loss by the changes proposed, showed themselves strongly adverse to the measure. The dissatisfaction soon found expression. Several members declared that unfair advantage was being taken of the panic into which the Colony had been thrown. The abolition of their long-standing and cherished independence of the Home authorities was being pressed with undue haste. Members had been brought

---

* The Rev. D. J. East's " Reminiscences." This sermon was afterwards published and reprinted by the Royal Commissioners in the Appendix to their Report.

together, not for consultation, but simply to attend
"the obsequies" of their free Constitution.   Honourable members in the higher offices had gone "rebellion
mad," and the Government had been frightened out
of their wits.   The statement that disaffection existed
throughout the island was an extravagant one, put
forth for the purpose of terrorising the Assembly.
Said one, "The handwriting is on the wall;" "we are
doomed.   He hoped," however, "that their dying
moments would be marked by something like decency,
and that they would go out of the world with credit
to themselves, respectably shrouded and respectably
buried." *

There was truth in these remonstrances.   In the
circular summoning the meeting of the Legislature,
the Governor had assured the members that they
might leave their homes with safety; and in the
resolution of thanks to General O'Connor and other
military officers, passed in the Privy Council held on
the 6th November, the day before the meeting of the
Assembly, His Excellency the Governor, with the
members of his Council, expressed the opinion "that
no reasonable cause now exists for expecting a continuance or revival of the late insurrection in the
eastern districts of the island"—that is, in the very
region of the outbreak.   Only three days before the
meeting of the Assembly, I find Mr. Eyre informing
the Secretary of State for the Colonies that the
General in command was of opinion that martial law

---

* Jamaica Parliamentary Debates for 1865, vol. xiii.

had become unnecessary, and that, though there had been a widespread feeling of disaffection, which, in a measure, still existed, there was "no organised combined action."

In the absence of colonial testimony to the terrible state of the island, as depicted by the Governor, we may fairly take his own valuation of its probable worth. Writing to Mr. Cardwell, on the 23rd December, he says: " In colonial communities fabrications and exaggerations of the grossest kind are constantly being circulated, either for sheer wantonness, or from a desire to appear important in the eyes of those to whom the statements are made, or from worse motives. These *canards* are very generally circulated by the local press, and often obtain currency and credence at a distance." *

Surely under such circumstances the House of Assembly should have been fully informed, and not driven, blindfolded by panic, or like scared sheep, to the " heroic " leap they were called upon so suddenly to make, " to offer on the altar of patriotism so great and generous a sacrifice," on which posterity should gaze "as a noble example of self-denial and heroism."

The history of this " Immolation " Bill may be dismissed in few words, for it was never in force. It was a very elaborate document, bearing the mark of prolonged deliberation, and having for its main object to replace the two branches of the Legislature by a single chamber, reducing the sixty-four members of

---

* Blue Book: Further Papers, Part II., p. 27.

the Constitution to twenty-four, one half of them to
be nominees of the Crown, and re-arranging the
entire machinery of administration under the general
supervision of the Colonial Office. It was read for the
first time in the House of Assembly on the 9th
November, and passed through all its stages by the
5th of December. On that day it was read the first
time in the Legislative Council, and passed its final
reading two days later, on the 7th, when it received
the approval of the Governor, and was transmitted
on the same day, so great was the haste to secure
the Royal Assent, to the Colonial Office, with a long
explanatory despatch from Mr. Eyre.

It was not a satisfactory measure even in the estimation of His Excellency. " It was a compromise,"
he states, " in which many details were admitted that
were disapproved by one section or the other." There
were also at work strong personal feelings, antagon-
istic to the men who would probably form the new
Executive, and only "patriotic feeling" induced the
Legislative Council to concur in the measure as finally
passed by the House of Assembly.

But now, in the most unexpected manner, the
scene suddenly underwent a remarkable transforma-
tion. Five days later, on the 12th December, a
message, transmitted through the Hon. Henry Westmorland, one of the three members of the Executive
Committee, was read, from the Governor, announcing
that so convinced were Her Majesty's Government of
the paramount importance of a strong government,
" that he had been confidentially informed (and which,

under existing circumstances, he feels justified in communicating to the Legislature) that **there** would be no
hesitation on the part of Her Majesty's **Government**
to accept any amount of additional responsibility
which circumstances might seem to require."

In consequence **of** this private information the
Governor respectfully invited "the Legislature **so to**
amend or rescind the Act, recently passed, as would
leave Her **Majesty unfettered** in determining **the**
character of the future Constitution, and the administrative machinery by which the business of the
country should be conducted." *

In reply to this message, so unexpectedly made
known to the Assembly, the House requested that
they might be furnished with a copy of the confidential despatch. To this Mr. Eyre replied that he
was unable to afford the House any further or more
definite information. He had received only a "private
and confidential intimation, **and** in general terms";
but he was assured that Her Majesty the Queen would
not **undertake** the responsibility of directing the affairs
of the Colony "**unless wholly unfettered**" in the creation of a new Constitution. **There was no help for it.**
The Jamaica Legislature was in a fix. **The surrender**
of the old Constitution—the Constitution granted by
the **Protector** Cromwell—must be absolute and un-
conditioned; **and so** great was the terror inspired by
Mr. Eyre's unproved assertions that, with only a few
remonstrances, the Act just **sent off** to the Colonial

---

* Parliamentary **Debates** of **Jamaica,** 1865, p. 151.

Office was rescinded, and a new Act, clear in its brevity, passed, surrendering the entire authority and government of the island into Her Majesty's hands. By the 21st of December the new and real Abolition Bill had passed both sections of the Legislature, and Her Majesty was endowed with the sole authority to "create and constitute a government" for the island, in such form as she pleased.*

If the new step was profoundly unwelcome to the governing classes of the community, the passing of this self-denying ordinance was hailed elsewhere with universal joy. "I was amused," says a resident in the island, "at the radiant looks of one of the most thoughtful gentlemen—not a Baptist—with whom I am acquainted, at the prospect of having legislative, administrative, parochial, and magisterial functions, all transferred into the hands of impartial men, sent out from Britain by the British Government. Now the thought is, we shall get on ; we shall have wisdom for unwisdom ; the general weal in preference to class interests, whether peasant or planter, black or white, and integrity and justice for corruption and jobbery. Now, too, it is believed, commercial confidence will be again restored, both here and at home. I am sure you will unite in the fervent prayer that these hopes may be realised."†

It was a surprising and unprecedented thing that a body of free men should surrender their power of self-government.   But some such issue had long been fore-

---

* Parliamentary Debates of Jamaica, 1865, p. 218.
† The *Freeman*, January 17th, 1866.

seen and desired in political circles in the mother
country. The old Charter had proved utterly
inapplicable to the changed condition of things. Its
abolition was the natural termination of "a vicious
career." The governing class in Jamaica had failed in
every way. It paid no heed to the warnings addressed
to it. Under its rule the island had been going from
bad to worse, and it was a just retribution that a Constitution, so scandalously used, should come to its end
by an act of political suicide. Surely the Governor
must have been laughing in his sleeve when he
characterised the deed as an "heroic act." It was a
shameful surrender of privileges which for nearly three
hundred years had been misused, a display of unfitness
for their enjoyment unparalleled in any free community. The Government of Jamaica had earned the
contempt of every thoughtful man, and deservedly
perished, "immolated" by its own hand.

The Legislature preserved to the end its character-
istic enmity to the coloured population. Within three
days of its assembling it passed an Act enabling
the Governor to detain persons arrested during
martial law, and another the effect of which was
to extend indefinitely its duration. Another Act
made it unlawful to administer or take unlawful
oaths, as if conspiracy was still rife, and gave the
power to inflict corporal punishment by the lash
for offences hitherto exempt. Other Bills were
brought in and discussed by this moribund body,
but which did not reach the dignity of Acts. Such
was a Bill which prohibited the importation of cut-

lasses, and other implements necessary in the ordinary occupations of the people. Another to embody the **Maroons as a** permanent **force,** for the repression of their **more** civilised fellows. **A** Liberal member of the House of **Assembly,** speaking **of** the course taken by **the Government, forcibly expressed** himself in **these terms :** "**Every Bill introduced by the** Executive cried **for more blood. In the name of all that** was sacred, what **could be** the **object of this measure,** except to provoke resistance from the masses? **Where** and how were all these proceedings to end ? All the House could learn from the Government, as their justification for daily bringing forward these bloody **measures, was, it was** necessary **to** strengthen **the hands of the Government, by** sending the police **and military among the quiet and** unoffending **peasantry, who were** peaceably pursuing their **work, to take the** implements **of labour out of** their **hands, and render** them furious." *

Under **the** pretence of preserving **the worship of** God from scandalous abuses, a Bill as intolerant as the persecuting Conventicle **Act of** Charles **II. was** introduced. It was a **blow** aimed especially at the Baptist ministers of the island ; and, in fact, included, with but one exception, all religionists who did not **belong to** the Church of England. A person pretending **to be** a minister **of** the Gospel **was** liable to **a heavy fine, or in** default to **an** imprisonment of two **years.** It **was even** provided that a person not

---

* **Mr.** Osborn's **Speech,** December 14th, **1865 :** Parliamentary Papers, **p. 174.**

leaving a place of worship within twenty minutes
after the conclusion of Divine worship, might be fined
£10, and not less than £1, and in default be committed to prison for three months with hard labour.
This intolerant measure was so far-reaching in its
operation that it would have prohibited the family
and students of the Calabar Theological Training
College from meeting together, according to custom,
for morning and evening worship. In vain did one or
two of the members of the Legislative Council protest
against a measure so repugnant to the principle of
liberty of religious worship. It was, however, read a
third time, and sent down to the House of Assembly.
After undergoing many modifications, it was finally
withdrawn.* This rendered unnecessary the opposition which awaited it in England. But it was an
evidence of the bitter spirit which to the last animated the Government of Jamaica, from the Governor
to its lowest officer, against the men who had been
the chief advocates of emancipation, and were its
jealous guardians so long as that Government endured.

The abolition of the Jamaica Constitution met
with the hearty concurrence of both political parties
in this country. In the discussion which ensued in
the House of Commons, on the 23rd February, on the
Bill presented by Mr. Cardwell ratifying the "abolition" Act of the Jamaica Legislature, Sir John
Pakington, on behalf of his party, said that he could

---

* Parliamentary Debates, p. 189.

have no doubt that it was his duty to support the measure of the Home Government. Under the circumstances, it was a necessary step; and not only so, the Jamaica Government itself " had abrogated their own functions, and declared their own unfitness and incapacity any longer to carry on the business of the Colony."

It was, undoubtedly, the general feeling of the nation that it would have been happier if the change of Constitution had been made at an earlier period, and this fine Colony saved from the state of decadence and ruin into which it had, through misgovernment, fallen.

CHAPTER VIII.

I NOW turn to the course of events in England following on the tidings of the disturbances and their suppression.

The intelligence of the outbreak reached me by the same mail that brought Mr. Eyre's despatch. Writing on the same day, the 16th November, to the Rev. J. M. Phillippo, and before I had seen Mr. Eyre's despatch, I thus expressed myself: " What shall I say about this most grievous and lamentable outbreak in St. Thomas-in-the-East, but that I am deeply grieved and shocked ? Not because your island papers throw the blame of it on my letter. On that score I have no regrets. My letter, now to become more famous than ever, was not addressed to the people of Jamaica. It was the Governor's act to give it the publicity it has acquired. But I grieve for the people who have lost their lives, and for the massacre in the name of justice which has followed it. The wickedness and folly of the few have been atoned for by the slaughter of multitudes. I can only console myself with the hope that our God will bring some good for Jamaica out of it. The state of things has been such

6*

as to demand great changes, and this will assuredly
hasten them."

On the same day, I wrote to the Rev. D. J. East :—

" The delay of the inward mail till within an hour
or two of post-time prevents me writing as I would
about this most lamentable outbreak. It gives
meaning to some of your letters, in which you say
that a strange feeling had come over the people. For
months past, I have felt that 'wrong' had eaten deep
into the hearts of the peasantry, and that, if something were not speedily done, it was quite possible
that the wilder and lawless spirits in the community
might break out into some overt act of revolt. Our
Government here has not been without some dread
of this, and scarcely six weeks ago, Mr. Cardwell
wrote me asking for an opinion as to what could at
once be done. I again urged, and at length, a Royal
Commission. But no step seems yet to have been
taken. The Government must now resolve on some
radical change in the mode of ruling Jamaica. If
that be the result of this sad and frightful event,
then good may come out of it. I hear that the revolt
is laid at my door by your island press. This I quite
expected when the first rumours of it reached this
country. Of course, the thing is absurd, and the
truth once known will quickly refute the charge. If
anyone is chargeable with it, it is Governor Eyre.
His unwise way of collecting materials for an answer
to Mr. Cardwell of necessity stirred the popular mind
to its depths. He excluded the coloured classes from
his appeal, and his placard added fuel to the flame.

I do not believe that Mr. Cardwell intended him to publish my letter; at least, there is no evidence that he did; and the state of things must have been bad indeed when the publication of it roused such an intense excitement throughout the island. At all events, Parliament will certainly take up the question of Jamaica's condition, and thus out of this dark and shocking event may come better days for the unfortunate island."

Mr. Eyre's despatch was not published in this country till Saturday, the 20th November, when it appeared in the *Times* newspaper, and in other papers in the week following. I was not till then aware of Mr. Eyre's accusations. The effect was startling. It immediately created an intense and widespread excitement, extending not only to political circles, but stirring the wonder and horror of all classes. To my astonishment I read that, in a great degree, "this most wicked and widespread rebellion" was due to Dr. Underhill's letter, to "Mr. G. W. Gordon, a member of Assembly, and a Baptist preacher," and to a few Baptist missionaries, "who endorsed at public meetings, and otherwise," all the untruthful statements or inuendoes propagated in Dr. Underhill's letter. This view was adopted after its own manner by a leading article in the *Times*. The nation was gravely informed that "in the old days of slavery, the Jamaica negro was noted among his race for his dangerous character, and that he rose against his masters, under the guidance of the Baptists, on the very eve of emancipation." And now again, "without the smallest provocation," and excited only by a fanatical hatred of the white man, they have broken out into murder and rapine. Thus the seven millions sterling paid in 1834 had only resulted in the ruin of the old proprietors, and to purchase for these 300,000 blacks "the liberty to squat, and maroon, or to hang about the towns of the island." It was added in bitter irony, "How all the efforts of philanthropy have ended may be read in our columns!" *

The despatch was read with astonishment and dismay, not only at the savage outbreak of the negro population, but at the cruel severity of the measures taken for its suppression. The more the appalling details were studied, the more frightful and ghastly did they appear. It was felt that the rising had been crushed with a violence and slaughter out of all proportion to the danger incurred. It was as if every vestige of humanity had been rooted out of the hearts and minds of the men, who revelled in the barbarities they inflicted on the panic-striken and fugitive wretches; on a foe that never once crossed a sword with them in fight, nor fired a musket at the men who slaughtered them like frightened sheep, and burnt their homesteads.

As the best answer to the *Times* article, and on the advice of friends, I sent to the newspapers my letter to Mr. Cardwell. It was no sooner published than letters full of sympathy began to crowd upon me from

---

* To this portion of the *Times* attack a reply was given by the Rev. Dr. Angus, but his letter was refused insertion. It was published in the *Daily News* of November 23rd.

all parts of the country. An irrepressible agitation sprang up throughout the land. I was urged to take advantage of a meeting in Camden Road Chapel, on the evening of the 20th of November, and again at Maidstone on the 27th, in order to explain the origin and nature of these painful events. The audiences were crowded and enthusiastic.

A similar meeting was held at Folkestone on the 21st, when the Rev. William Arthur gave his impressive testimony against the shocking crimes related by the very men to whom the repression of the "rebellion" was entrusted. From this time public meetings multiplied in all parts of the land, at many of which I was invited to be present. In almost all cases they were called by requisition to the mayors, and often met under their presidency.

Among the most important places that expressed their horror of the statements of the military authorities, and called upon the Government for immediate intervention and inquiry, were Newcastle, Brighton, York, Shields, Manchester, Plymouth, Leeds, Bradford, Reading, Derby, Rochdale, and many others too numerous to mention. A most impressive deputation was appointed by Manchester to wait on the Secretary of State. It was quickly followed by a larger body, the Anti-Slavery Society, which gathered from its thirty branches a deputation consisting of more than two hundred and fifty delegates. They saw Mr. Cardwell on Saturday, the 9th December. They besought the Government to take immediate steps "for an impartial and searching inquiry into the deplorable events which have recently occurred in Jamaica, and the causes which have occasioned them." In the memorial they presented they briefly recount the facts as set forth in Mr. Eyre's despatches, and affirm that there was no evidence of a malevolent purpose on the part of the rioters. While they condemn the outrages committed by an infuriated populace, they regard the firing of the Volunteers into the mob as a rash and unwarrantable act, and the indiscriminate massacre of the coloured people by the soldiers, sailors, and the maroons, when all serious apprehension of further disturbances had ceased, as a proceeding deserving of the strongest reprobation. The people were hunted down in their own districts, the majority of whom were unarmed and not implicated in the riot. The proceedings against Mr. Gordon and his execution, they say, were flagrantly illegal. They close their memorial by a brief reference to the antecedent discontent, and to the unjust administration of the laws in Jamaica.

To the profound gratification of the large assembly before him, Mr. Cardwell stated that Her Majesty's Government had anticipated their request, and "had determined that there should be forthwith a full, an impartial, and an independent inquiry." Arrangements, he said, were already in progress, and information of them would go to Jamaica by the next mail ; but he desired that the conduct of Mr. Eyre and the authorities should not be prejudged.

CHAPTER IX.

GEORGE WILLIAM GORDON.

NO incident of the dreadful story narrated in the despatches forwarded by Governor Eyre produced a more painful impression than the arrest, trial, and execution of Mr. G. W. Gordon. He was a half-caste by birth, but a man of property, of good education and standing in society, married to an English wife, and of a religious habit of mind.* He was one of the few coloured men who had found their way into the House of Assembly. He was member for the district in which the outbreak took place. For many years before the arrival of Governor Eyre he had held the position of magistrate, but was displaced by Mr. Eyre, on account of a dispute which arose out of the case of a negro whom Mr. Gordon had befriended, believing him to be unjustly and cruelly treated. Though the act of the Governor was not reversed, the Duke of Newcastle, the then Colonial Minister, required an apology to Mr. Gordon to be made by Mr. Eyre. It was reluctantly and grudg-

---

* Some years before these events he had been baptized by the Rev. J. M. Phillippo; but he did not join the Baptist denomination.

ingly done, and left in both parties much sore feeling behind. During the administration of Mr. Eyre many other causes of offence had sprung up, in which Mr. Gordon had taken a leading part. He was often an opponent of the Governor's measures in the Assembly,* and a staunch and unfailing advocate of the interests of the negro, to which race, by his birth he was allied. He had also interested himself in the land disputes, which stirred up so much discontent in and around Morant Bay, where he himself also possessed a small estate.†

With the excitement that followed the publication of my letter Mr. Gordon deeply sympathised. He presided at the "Underhill Meeting" held in Kingston on May 3rd,‡ in the absence of the Mayor, saying but a few introductory words on the general object of the meeting. He was believed to be the author of the placard calling, with the consent of the Custos, an "Underhill Meeting" at Morant Bay. Here he spoke more at length. He reminded the people of the heavy taxation to which they were subject, their destitute and forlorn condition, the oppressive conduct of the Custos and local magistracy, which, he said, was sufficient to extinguish the patience with which hitherto it had been borne,

---

* He was regarded by Mr. Eyre as "the most consistent and untiring obstructor of the public business in the House of Assembly." Despatch, May 17th, 1865. Papers, &c., p. 192.

† "Personal Recollections of the Hon. G. W. Gordon," by the Rev. Duncan Fletcher. Chap. vi., p. 80.

‡ Report of the Royal Commission, p. 278.

and he energetically urged his fellow-citizens to remonstrate, strongly and earnestly, against it. But he advised no violent action.

He took no part in the rising or its immediate antecedents. At the time of its occurrence he was in Kingston, many miles away. His active interest in public life, and close intimacy with the affairs of the parish of St. Thomas-in-the-East, naturally led many to associate his name with the names of the actors in the outbreak.˙ So that when, on October 12th, the news of it reached Kingston, the authorities determined to treat him as a guilty party. He resided usually at a short distance from the town of Kingston, but had a place of business there. For three or four days before his arrest he was occupied with his business as usual; but his friends urged him to absent himself for a short time. Conscious of his innocence, he positively refused. "If," he said, "it is for the tranquillity of the country, I will keep myself quiet for a day or two, but to go away to make myself guilty I never will." * Hearing, however, that a warrant had been issued for his arrest, on Tuesday, October 17th, he voluntarily proceeded to the office of the commander of the troops. He was then and there placed under arrest, by the Governor in person and the Custos of Kingston. The city of Kingston, by a special resolution of the Privy Council, had been exempted from the operation of martial law which covered the county of Surrey. The Lord Chief Justice

* "The Case of G. W. Gordon," by B. T. Williams, Esq., Barrister-at-Law, 1866, p. 22.

of England, in his celebrated charge, distinctly states that these two gentlemen " were not the ministers or apparitors of the martial authority, and did not possess the power to take up Mr. Gordon for the purpose of handing him over to the martial law. Nevertheless, they did it. They did it by the exercise of the strong hand of power, because it was thought that a conviction could not be got at Kingston. It was altogether unlawful and unjustifiable. To Mr. Gordon it made the difference of life or death." * It deprived him of the means and opportunity of self-defence and legal assistance.

Mr. Eyre must have been well aware of the illegality of the course taken.† He says himself in his despatch :—" Great difference of opinion prevailed in Kingston as to the policy of taking Mr. Gordon." But he argued that, as Mr. Gordon was "the chief instigator of all the evils that had taken place, and there was fear of an outbreak in Kingston, he deemed it right in the abstract, and desirable as a matter of policy, not to let the chief rebel escape punishment ; so I at once took upon myself the responsibility of his capture." ‡

---

* Charge of the Lord Chief Justice of England, *In re The Queen* v. *Nelson and Brand*, London, 1867, p. 114.

† It appears from the evidence of Mr. Westmorland, one of Mr. Eyre's Executive Council, that he suggested at the time that Mr. Gordon should be reserved for trial by a regular—*i.e.* civil—tribunal, by which the means of defence are secured by ordinary process of law. (" Case of W. G. Gordon," by B. T. Williams, p. 23.)

‡ Papers relating to the Disturbances, &c., Part I., p. 6. Despatch of October 20th, 1865.

In a later despatch, dated January, 1866, Mr. Eyre distinctly recognises the illegality of his act, but he trusted to obtain an " Act of Indemnity" to cover his deviation from a strictly legal course, which he secured prior to the final abolition of the Constitution. *

Without further delay, about noon on the day of capture, the Governor, with a supply of arms and ammunition, took his captive on board the steamer *Wolverine*, and sailed for Morant Bay.

On Friday, the 20th, he set Mr. Gordon with other prisoners on shore, and committed him to the custody of Provost Marshal Ramsay. The intervening days had been spent by the Governor visiting places on the coast, precious days lost to Mr. Gordon, which might have been occupied in preparation for his trial.

The crucial importance of this detention in custody on board the steamer by the Governor, will be best understood from the issue of at least one attempt during the time to aid the prisoner in his anticipated trial. Prohibited access to Mr. Gordon, a letter was addressed to him, " A prisoner on H.M.S. *Wolverine*," by Mr. Wemys Anderson, of Tichfield, enclosed in an open state to Brigadier Nelson, who controlled all the proceedings of the courts-martial at Morant Bay, and which came into the Brigadier's possession previous to the trial. In this valuable and most important letter, Mr. Anderson states that he knew nothing of the charges about to be brought against Gordon ; but, " as

* Further Papers, Part II., p. 195.
† See "Report of the Royal Commission," p. 795.

an old friend and professional adviser," he could not refrain from tendering his advice. Whatever errors Mr. Gordon may have committed *before* the proclamation of martial law, "he advised him to plead," first, that you are answerable only to the ordinary civil and criminal courts of the country; and second, that " that only is crime which is prompted by criminal intention, and that you, having no such intention, are not criminally liable for the consequences, however disastrous they unhappily may have been."

That letter never reached the prisoner. It was read and destroyed by Brigadier Nelson.

At length, on the morning of Friday, the 20th, to quote Mr. Eyre's despatch, " having landed Brigadier Nelson, and the Militia officers who aided as members of courts-martial, and having put on shore the prisoners, including G. W. Gordon, I again proceeded in the *Wolverine* to Kingston, reaching that city about 2 p.m." Thus was Gordon left to his fate. He was imprisoned in the police-station, in the charge of the Provost Marshal. During his confinement on board the *Wolverine*, and afterwards in the police-office, Mr. Gordon was labouring under great infirmity; he had no coat on, "he had a blanket which he wrapped on his shoulders and it hung down." *

The Brigadier found a considerable mass of documents, awaiting his perusal, from which to select such evidence as existed of Gordon's criminality to guide the Provost Marshal, who acted as prosecutor on behalf

---

* " Papers Relating to the Disturbances," Part I., p. 7.

of the Government. The Court-Martial was composed of two Lieutenants of the Royal Navy, and an
Ensign of the 4th West India Regiment. The Court
assembled at two o'clock on Saturday, the 21st, Lieu-
tenant-Commander Brand acting as President. Care
was taken to exclude all persons friendly to the
prisoner.

The President read the charges, which were as
follows. I take them as stated in the Report of the
Royal Commission :—

"The charges against the prisoner were for furthering the massacre at Morant Bay, and at divers periods
previously inciting and advising with certain insurgents, and there by his influence tending to cause the
riot. Two heads of offence were drawn up, one for
High Treason, the other for complicity with certain
parties engaged in the rebellion, riot, and insurrection
at Morant Bay." *

Such were the charges. About four hours and
a half were occupied in the trial, of which an
hour was employed by the prisoner in his defence.
Five witnesses were sworn and examined for the
prosecution, and one, living on the spot, was summoned on behalf of the prisoner.

How evidence was obtained may be imagined by
the following statement, given to the Royal Commission on oath by Joseph Gordon Smith, a volunteer of
Astwood's troop.

---

* I have taken this *précis* of the Trial from the report published in Jamaica, in 1866, by A. W. H. Lake. It may also be
found in the Report of the Royal Commission, p. 277.

"I went," he says, "with a number of prisoners, to Morant Bay. Ramsay flogged them without even asking their names. Afterwards I went to the guard-room, and he was then swearing five of them, with their hands fastened and a rope round their necks; and he was swearing them in these words: 'You shall well and truly state what G. W. Gordon has to do with the rebellion'; and between each part of this a sailor came down with the whip over their shoulders." * Under such circumstances, it will be interesting to give a brief sketch of the evidence laid before the Court.

The first witness for the prosecution was a black man, a schoolmaster and a rebel, John Anderson by name, who had been hunted up by the Provost Marshal from the mass of prisoners in his hands. He stated that he had seen Mr. Gordon at Stony Gut on a Sunday, about the month of June or July, and that he had been present at a meeting in August, near the Court House. Gordon said to Bogle that if the back lands were not obtained they must all die. He knew Mr. Gordon quite well. Some resolutions were passed at this meeting which dealt with the degraded state of the people and the base treatment of the labourers; but no suggestions were made of violent reprisals or insurrection. This was the strongest evidence against Gordon adduced at the trial.

The next witness, James Gordon, was a black man

---

* Report, p. 54.

and a rebel. A deposition was put in, taken in the presence of the Inspector of Prisons. It was to the effect that Mr. G. W. Gordon had sent a letter to the Valley stating there would be war, that the people must prepare for it, and that then they would get their land free. Cross-examined, he said he knew the letter came from Mr. Gordon, but he did not know the signature; only from the contents he knew it came from him. Mr. Gordon remarked in reply, "I never wrote such a letter in my life."

Next was tendered the dying confession of a rebel, by name Thomas Williams. It stated that Gordon said all the outside land should be got for nothing. He held two meetings. At Stony Gut all the people were Gordon's friends. Mr. Gordon's people made the disturbances, and "he teach them." The prisoner observed, "All this is given on hearsay, and I deny it all."

The Provost Marshal then tendered a document signed by two men named Peart and Humber, of the parish of Vere,* sworn before a Justice of Peace in the same parish. It purported to contain a portion of a speech delivered by Gordon at an " Underhill Meet-

---

* The Royal Commissioners state that Peart and Humber were in Jamaica at the time of the trial, and might have been summoned to give oral testimony. They were of the class between which and the negroes there was constant strife, on account of wages, &c. Chevannes and Thomas also were living in Jamaica. Their written statements were taken in the absence of Gordon, and were inadmissible in English courts, either civil or military. (Report, p. 36.) This, too, was the opinion of Lord Cockburn. (Charge, p. 126.)

ing" in Vere. Gordon was said to have declared the
Governor to be a bad man, who sanctions everything
done by the white man to the oppression of the black
man. "The friends of Mr. Eyre represent to the
Queen that you are thieves. The 'Queen's Advice'
is all trash! It is not her advice." You work on
Sundays. Sabbath-breaking is bringing down a curse
on you. "Do as they do in Haiti." The prisoner
remarked: "As to Haiti, I never thought it, and my
Heavenly Father knows it." *

A letter was next handed to the Court, seized in
the house of the rebel Chisholm, which he swore was
in the handwriting of Gordon. The only sentence in
it of any importance, was a statement that "the
people are all starving in Vere; pray to God for help
and deliverance." † He regarded Mr. Gordon as a
peacemaker.

There seems to have been no reason why the three
persons last mentioned were not produced in Court
for cross-examination.

The next following evidence was a deposition made
by Charles Chevannes before a police magistrate,
stating that after the trial of the case of "*Gordon* v.
The Baron," in which Gordon was worsted, he said,

---

* Dr. Bruce, who was at the meeting, and sat close to Gordon,
with others, deny that Gordon used these words about Haiti.
(Report, p. 32.) On the 12th September, therefore long before
the trial, Gordon denied in the *Guardian* that he used the
expression.

† The Court seem to have made no inquiry into the genuine-
ness of any of the documents. (Report, 633, 653.) "I asked no
questions," said Lieut. Bray (p. 654).

Never mind; if 1 don't get revenge, my people will."

Another deposition was next handed in, made by George Thomas, lying sick in the hospital, within 130 yards of the Court-Martial. So far as it affected the accused, the purport of it was that Gordon never came to the meetings of Bogle and his friends; but that by letter he told Bogle that the lands were going to be free, and put up Bogle to do all this rebellion. "Mr. Gordon was the head of the rebellion. I have heard Mr. Gordon advise the people not to pay for the lands." The prisoner's reply was simply, "That is quite untrue." *

The Court had next laid before them three hundred copies of a placard, which was simply a notice, with blanks, of a meeting to be held (blank) for the purpose of (blank), and so on.

Another placard produced was supposed to be printed at the *Watchman* office, and was headed, "The State of the Island." † It announced a public meeting at Morant Bay on the 29th July, urging the people to attend. The postmistress of Kingston was called to give evidence respecting it. Elizabeth Jane Gough said it was one of two papers addressed

---

* Lieutenant Brand swore before the Commission that he did not ask where Thomas was, who made the deposition, or whether he could be brought into Court. Thomas swore before the Royal Commission that he was quite capable of giving his evidence in person. He had a wound in the shoulder, but nothing was the matter with his legs. (Report, p. 655.)

† See Report of Commission, p. 31.

7*

to Bogle and Chisholm, in the handwriting of Gordon. A letter was shown to her, which she also swore was in Mr. Gordon's handwriting, and signed by him. She had taken the placard out of the wrapper.

(In the sworn evidence of George Sharp, given before the Royal Commission,* he stated that he was a compositor in Mr. Gordon's employ, and that three packets of the above placard were addressed by him to Bogle, Chisholm, and Sullivan.)

James McLaren, a rebel prisoner under sentence of death, was examined on oath. To the question, "Do you know Mr. Gordon has something to do with the rebellion?" he replied, "I know I am going to be hanged this night; I don't know if he has anything to do with it." To the prisoner's question, "Have I ever sent up to tell you to get up a subscription, and not to pay for the lands, and to get up a rebellion, or to advise them to any improper act?" the witness answered, "No. I heard him (G. W. Gordon) at the public meeting on the 12th of August advise me and others to pay my taxes."

The Provost Marshal finally handed in a letter from the prisoner to a Mr. E. C. Smith, in which he lamented the death of Mr. Hire, and attributed it to the arbitrary power of the Baron, adding, "People can't hope for justice. This is the true cause of the discontent." The prisoner admitted this to be his writing, but added, "There was no intent there."

---

* Report, pp. 905 and 1041. Sharp also testified that he received the paper headed "The State of the Island" from Mr. Gordon to set up.

Here the evidence for the prosecution closed. To say it was inconclusive is to minimise its worthlessness; it was morally and intrinsically bad. It was evidence which neither by the ordinary nor military law ought to have been admitted. It was utterly contrary to the rules of right or justice. There was, in fact, no evidence to warrant the allegation that Mr. Gordon was an accomplice of the rebels.*

The only witness available for the prisoner was a man called to speak to Mr. Gordon's illness, as the cause of his absence from the Vestry on the 11th October. A Dr. Major, whom he wished to call, was declared by Ramsay to be absent from the Bay.†

The prisoner was then called upon for his defence. In a speech of about an hour's duration, marked by some natural hesitation of manner and great debility, for he had been kept standing during the whole of the trial, he referred first to the circumstances of his arrest, as already given. He then expressed his regard for Europeans, being brought up among them, and his desire for the education of the people by their agency. Possessed of much land, he could have no interest in promoting rebellion. He had endeavoured

---

* Lord Cockburn's Charge, pp. 115 and 119.

† It was subsequently ascertained that Dr. Major was in Morant Bay, but that the desire of Gordon to call him as a witness was wilfully kept from his knowledge. The absence of Gordon from the Vestry on the day of the outbreak was regarded as a conclusive proof of his knowledge of what was about to take place. Dr. Major could have disproved this; hence the denial of his presence in Morant Bay on the day of the trial.

to secure the franchise for the black people, that in a legitimate manner reforms might be secured. " And I solemnly, before my Maker and this Court, declare that I never knew from Paul Bogle or any other person in this parish of an intended insurrection. I knew nothing of it until I was informed by a policeman in Kingston. I never heard from any of the parties of their movements or intentions in the least degree. Circumstantial evidence may be suspicious on me, but I can't help that." He finally referred to the words attributed to him about Haiti as incorrect. " I solemnly declare I never thought of Haiti when I was at the meeting at Vere; and those words, supposing them to be correct, were spoken in another parish, having nothing to do with this." He concluded his defence with these words : "I hope it may be the pleasure of the Court to take further information. No charge is made against me for being concerned in any rebellion. I had expected, if any crime or misdemeanour were charged against me, I should have been tried on the merits in Kingston ; and as I was not taken up in any rebellious act, nor on rebel ground, neither within any martial-law district, I freely gave myself up to His Excellency the Governor so soon as I heard that suspicions were held against me." This pathetic appeal was without effect.

After half an hour's deliberation the Court adjourned.

My readers will readily perceive the worthlessness of the evidence on which this excellent man was adjudged to death. It will suffice to quote the conclusion formed respecting it, in the impartial and patient investigation of the Royal Commission. "The evidence, oral and documentary, appears to us to be wholly insufficient to establish the charge upon which the prisoner took his trial."

This mockery of a trial came to a close about half-past seven, after "set of sun," and in the following laconic words Brigadier Nelson announced to his superior officer the finding of the Court: "The sentence was death." But before the victim could be informed, the finding had to receive the approval of the authorities, and the Sabbath day was spent in forwarding the papers to Kingston, and in securing their assent.

At six p.m. on Sunday evening, Governor Eyre wrote to Nelson * : "Your report of the trial of George William Gordon has just reached me through the General, and I quite concur in the justice of the sentence, and the necessity of carrying it into effect." At ten minutes past seven on Monday morning, so precise is the language of the despatch, Mr. Gordon was informed of the doom awaiting him, and at eight o'clock the dread sentence was carried into effect."†

He occupied the brief hour allowed him, in writing to his wife, a few sentences from which deserve to be quoted :—

---

* Papers, &c., Part I., p. 24.

† He was hung by two or three sailors from the centre of the ruined arch of the Court House. Lieut. Errington, one of the members of the Court-Martial which condemned Gordon, was in command of the men by whom he was hung. (Report, p. 663.

" My Beloved Lucy,—General Nelson has just been kind enough to inform me that the Court-Martial on Saturday last has ordered me to be hung, and that the sentence is to be executed in an hour hence, so that I shall be gone from this world of sin and sorrow. I do not deserve this sentence, for I never advised or took part in any insurrection. All I ever did was to recommend the people who complained to seek redress in a legitimate way; and if in this I erred, or have been misrepresented, I do not think I deserve the extreme sentence. It is, however, the will of my Heavenly Father that I should thus suffer in obeying His command to relieve the poor and needy, and to protect, as far as I am able, the oppressed. . . .

"The judges seemed against me; and from the rigid manner of the Court, I could not get in all the explanations I intended. The man, Anderson, made an unfounded statement, and so did Gordon, but his testimony was different from the deposition. The judges took the former and erased the latter. It seemed that I was to be sacrificed. I know nothing of Bogle, and never advised him to the act or acts which have brought upon me this end. . . .

" I did not expect that, not being a rebel, I should have been tried and disposed of in this way. I thought His Excellency the Governor would have allowed me a fair trial if any charge of sedition or inflammatory language were justly attributable to me, but I have no power of control. May the Lord be merciful to him. . . .

" Now, my dearest one, the most beloved and

faithful one, the Lord bless, help, preserve, and keep you." *

An eminent journalist at the time thus sums up the case of Mr. Gordon :—" It is not alleged that Mr. Gordon was taken with arms in his hands, though even that would not justify his trial by Court-Martial, unless he was taken in a district which was at that time under martial law; and according to English law, a military court has no jurisdiction to try a non-military subject of the Crown for any offence whatever, other than armed resistance to the authorities in a proclaimed district. The Brigadier-General and the officers who sat on that Court-Martial, and the soldiers who carried their sentence into effect, have one and all been guilty of wilful murder." †

Such was the judgment formed at the time by eminent jurists, and held for truth by vast numbers of the people of Great Britain. It cannot be remembered but with the deepest regret that a man estimable in some respects, a Governor of an English Colony, should have allowed his personal feelings to prompt him to take so prominent a share in the arrest and prosecution unto death of a man who, if too strongly

---

* Fletcher's " Personal Recollections," p. 125.

† The *Solicitors' Journal.* Even the *Times* gives their Jamaica correspondent (March 30th) credit for saying :—" I may as well express here my opinion that no evidence has been given to prove either that Mr. Gordon could have been legally convicted of complicity with the rioters or rebels of Morant Bay, or that there was anything like organisation among the negroes throughout the island with a view to rebel."

sensitive to the oppression of the race to which he belonged, was actuated in the main by humane and Christian motives. " I can say," were his dying words, " it is a great honour thus to suffer in such a cause, for the servant cannot be greater than his Lord."

The view here taken of Mr. Gordon's case, finds its fullest and final justification in the remarkable language of the Lord Chief Justice of England, in the summing-up of his charge to the Grand Jury in the case of " The Queen against Nelson and Brand," in the Central Criminal Court of the Old Bailey, on the 10th April, 1867. *

After contrasting the treatment in Mr. Gordon's case with that of the Fenian prisoners at Dublin by Mr. Justice Fitzgerald, Lord Cockburn proceeds to say :—

" Taken from a place where he would have had the advantage of a regular trial, a previous knowledge of the case he had to meet, the means of defence, the presence of friends, the assistance of counsel, the cross-examination of the witnesses, the full opportunity to rebut their testimony by counter - evidence, the direction to the jury of a professional and responsible judge, he is hurried off without an opportunity of communicating with anyone, and transported to another part of the island, where he had neither friend nor adviser. Even a letter written to him by a friend suggesting the line of defence is purposely kept

---

* " Charge of the Lord Chief Justice of England," revised and corrected ; edited by Frederick Cockburn, Esq., of the Crown Office (London : Ridgway, 1867), p. 164.

from him. Alone and helpless, he is immediately, and with unseemly and deplorable haste, put upon his trial, without knowledge of the charge till called upon to answer it, without knowledge of the facts intended to be proved, or of the witnesses intended to be examined, still less that the depositions of living witnesses taken behind his back would be brought forward against him. Under these most disadvantageous circumstances he is put upon his trial, before a court in all probability sharing in the common prepossession against him, and is condemned on evidence, in my judgment, wholly insufficient to warrant his condemnation.

"It may be said, it is true, that Gordon did not apply for a postponement of the trial. But of what advantage would a postponement have been to him while in total ignorance of what he had to meet? Besides which, this unhappy man appears, if one may judge from the utter want of vigour and intelligence displayed in his defence, to have been paralysed by the circumstances in which he was placed, and to have been rendered incapable of grappling with the difficulties by which he was surrounded. No one, I think, who has the faintest idea of what the administration of justice involves, could deem the proceedings on this trial consistent with justice, or, to use a homely phrase, with that fair play which is the right of the commonest criminal. All I can say is that if, on martial law being proclaimed, a man can lawfully be thus tried, condemned, and sacrificed, such a state of things is a scandal and a reproach to the institutions

of this great and free country; and as a minister of
justice, profoundly imbued with a sense of what is
due to the first and greatest of earthly obligations, I
enter my solemn and emphatic protest against the
lives of men being thus dealt with in the time to
come."

I shall not be doing full justice to Mr. Gordon's
memory if I do not add a few extracts from a letter
I received from him, dated September 8th, a month
before the outbreak, clearly showing that he had no
part in or expectation of a violent explosion of the
existing discontent :—

"I have had a great deal to do with meetings convened to consider your letter, and a circular sent by
Mr. Cardwell to Mr. Eyre, which the latter has issued
as 'The Queen's Advice.' This document is exten-
sively circulated, and sent to all ministers of religion.
By several it has been accepted and read in the
churches for effect, so that the poor people think there
is no hope for them. The planters rejoice over it, and
seem delightfully encouraged in their unreasonable-
ness and oppression. The condition of the people
continues deplorable, and nowhere that I have been
more so than in the parish of Vere, where a meeting
was held on Monday, the 4th July. The state of
matters here is really serious—children naked and
starving, and coolies too; adults in misery, and not
having raiment even to come to the meeting; and
from these causes the places of worship are nearly
empty, and the schools badly attended, so that in
point of fact the social fabric is fast giving way."

He then relates the sad details of a case at "The Alley," and continues:—"The magistrates are principally all overseers, of a very inferior class of men, and they sit in judgment on the labourers employed by themselves, and it becomes the law of terror and oppression."

"As to the poor people, they have no chance with the Governor when they complain of wrong and oppression; and all this really exists in Jamaica. After the labourers have worked, the planter-magistrates make all possible objections and refuse to pay, and the people have virtually no redress."

"Were Mr. Eyre a gentleman, and a man of considerate feelings, one would endeavour to confer with him; but it is hopeless. He is prejudiced and ill-disposed. We must depend on Divine interposition. Something must be done, and it occurs to me that our people would do even better in America as soon as matters are settled there."

CHAPTER X.

THE atrocities of the suppression acquired additional horror by the employment of the Maroons. These semi-civilised negroes are the descendants of original runaway slaves, at the time when the island was in the occupation of the Spaniards. Living in the fastnesses of the mountains, they resisted subjugation when the island fell into the hands of the English, and were increased in numbers, from time to time, by fugitives from the sugar and coffee plantations. About the year 1838 they acknowledged the British rule, but were permitted to retain their own officers, laws, and customs, under a white superintendent. To Colonel Fyfe, a former governor amongst them, was given the command of a body numbering about seventy or a hundred men, who came to Bath offering themselves for enlistment. On the 19th October, under orders from Governor Eyre, arms were provided for them by Brigadier Nelson,

Sudden and rapid in their movements, undisciplined and unencumbered with commissariat, these rude denizens of the mountains were deemed suitable allies in hunting the rebels, and in tracing them to their hiding places. They were sent off to scour the country, to break into the dwellings of supposed rebels, shooting captives without trial, and burning their homesteads on the most insufficient evidence, or no evidence at all, of complicity in the outbreak. Many prisoners were also taken and placed in the hands of the military. Some of the rebels, it was stated, were Obeahmen, dealers in magic and secret arts, and on that account alone worthy of death. In these excursions many persons were shot, and 140 cottages destroyed by fire. A grand banquet was finally given them, in Kingston, on the 13th November, to celebrate their exploits, and to receive the thanks of the Governor.

A large number of persons were arrested at various times, in places both within and without the sphere of martial law, and on its cessation were detained in custody for trial before a Special Commission of Oyer and Terminer formed in Kingston, the legality of which was subject to the gravest question. The members of the Court were selected specially for their known hostility to the coloured race. The prisoners, with few exceptions, were accused of "felonious riot." On trial some were declared not guilty; but the majority were convicted on the most flimsy evidence, and sentenced to various terms of penal servitude, some for life and others for twenty years. But the following cases deserve special mention from the position and estimable character of the men.*

* Report of Royal Commission, p. 25.

E. J. Goldson **was** arrested **in** Kingston.   **He had
been for** eleven years in the police force, in which he
had attained the rank **of** sergeant.   On his arrest, he
was first tried **for using seditious** words at the
" Underhill Meeting " on **the 3rd May.   As** the jury
could **not** agree, **after six days'** detention **he** was
discharged.   **On the** 19th **October he was** again
arrested, without **a** warrant, and taken **to the bar-**
racks, and thence to the Up Park Camp.   **His jailer**
examined him.   He denied that he was a friend **of**
Mr. Gordon, and said that at the meeting he had
spoken only against the **law** of assault.   He was,
however, taken **on board the** *Aboukir*, with his hands
tied to his back, and **so tight as to** cause excruciating
pain.   He was put into irons, and so remained **from
Saturday to Tuesday, exposed** to the foulest abuse
from the soldiery.   **On the 1st** November, he was
removed to the *Cordelia* for transport to Morant Bay.
Here he was given in custody **to Provost** Marshal
Ramsay, who, seeing him, asked, " What **is that man**
doing there ? "   He was taken out, stripped, lashed to
a post in the street, and flogged by a white soldier.
A policeman was ordered to flog him, but he refused.
After suffering other indignities, **he was** released on
the 26th **by a writ of** Habeas Corpus, when he returned
to Kingston.   **He was** afterwards charged before the
Commission **Court and tried for** conspiracy.   He was
acquitted.*

The Rev. J. H. Crole, **a fair, brown man,** a native

* **Report of Royal Commission, p. 310.**

Baptist minister connected with Mr. Gordon's Taber-
nacle, was another of these victims of injustice. He
was fellow-prisoner with Goldson and Kelly Smith,
and transhipped with them to Morant Bay. His
companion, Kelly Smith, thus describes what he
saw: " The perspiration was running down his face."
Ramsay said: " That man is winking at his fellow-
prisoner; take him out, and give him a dozen." He
said " he was not doing anything." Ramsay said:
" Give him another dozen for saying that." He had
one dozen. They were about to tie him again, and
some gentlemen outside interfered by some sort of
sign, and Crole was released, to the amazement of the
police and others.* He was subsequently tried by
the Commission Court for using seditious language
at the " Underhill Meeting," of May 3rd.

Mr. Kelly Smith, part editor of the *Watchman*, was
also a companion in tribulation; and, though he
escaped the lash, he had to endure a severe imprisonment, and was daily made to witness the numerous
executions which took place. His friends obtained a
writ of Habeas Corpus, and he returned to Kingston,
where he was tried for conspiracy, and acquitted.†

Mr. Sidney Levien, editor of the *County Union*, an
opposition paper, published in Kingston, was also
arrested during the reign of terror. For fifteen years
he had creditably filled the post of editor. His crime

---

* Report of Royal Commission, p. 195: Kelly Smith's
evidence.

† Further Correspondence relative to the Affairs of Jamaica,
p. 73.

8

consisted of an article, in which he declared that the
outbreak was the natural consequence of Mr. Eyre's
misgovernment, his disregard of justice in his treatment of Mr. G. W. Gordon, his failure to give reasonable support to native industry, and his general
neglect of duty. These statements were interspersed
with some personal allusions to the Governor's private
habits. For this article, however (if there was any
other offence, it was not stated), he was arrested, put
in prison, and sent to Morant Bay, which place he had
styled a "Gehenna," and the "Valley of Death." His
trial did not, however, come on during martial law,
nor do we know whether it could have taken place
under the clauses of the new Act passed by the
Legislature then in session. He found means to bring
his arrest and detention under the consideration of
the Civil Court, and before judges trained in the
principles of English law. The result was that the
Chief Justice discharged him from custody, on the
express ground that the Act of the Legislature was
unconstitutional, and gave a power to the Governor
which ought not to be entrusted to anyone in his
position. He also stated that, for his arrest, Mr.
Levien might obtain redress. He was, however, again
arrested, and tried before Sir Bryan Edwards under the
same Commission as Palmer and others. He was convicted and confined in the Surrey Jail. Sir John
Peter Grant, after his arrival in Jamaica as Governor,
offered him a free pardon, which he declined to accept.
He was, however, subsequently released.

One other case deserves further mention, that of the

Rev. Edwin Palmer, a black man and minister of the Baptist Church meeting in Hanover Street, Kingston. Though a coloured man, he had received a good education.

As my readers already know, martial law was not proclaimed over the city of Kingston, where Mr. Palmer lived, and where there was not the least sign of rebellion or sympathy with the atrocities that had been committed elsewhere. With other peaceful inhabitants, Mr. Palmer was arrested, without any warrant, on the 20th October, by the order of the Governor. Of the crime with which he was accused he was kept in perfect ignorance. After being detained in the city cage for some hours, he was conveyed to the barracks, and placed in a dark cell. The day following, under military escort, he was removed to the Up Park Camp. Here he was stripped of his boots, his hair cut, his hands tied behind him, and locked up in a cell. The next day, guarded by a large military escort, with muskets loaded and bayonets fixed, he was led through the city of Kingston to the Ordnance Wharf, and delivered into the custody of the master gunner of the guardship *Aboukir*. He was put in irons by the captain, and remained in that condition from Saturday night until Tuesday, the 24th. The cruelties inflicted upon him induced a high state of fever, and for a few hours partially unhinged his mind; but under the direction of the ship's doctor he was relieved of his irons and brought on deck, and recovered. On the 2nd November he was placed on board H.M.S. *Cordelia*, and taken to Morant Bay.

8*

With his fellow-prisoner Goldson, **he was** handed
over to **Provost** Marshal Ramsay, **and** was instantly
marched to the police-station ; and on his way thither,
amidst the taunts and jeers of the marines, he was
shown the gallows and ropes all prepared, he was told,
for his execution **at seven o'clock the** next morning.
Goldson **was** lashed to a post **and flogged, also** Samuel
Clark, who on the following day **was hung. For some**
unknown reason, though foully and wickedly **abused**
as a " Baptist parson " by the Provost Marshal, and as
a " black devil," fit only to be a hewer of wood and
drawer of water, Palmer was left unwhipped, but was
constantly **ordered on parade to witness the** frequent
executions. In all this there was an entire disregard
of sex or age, the innocent or the guilty, and an utter
recklessness **with regard to the** taking away of human
life. It is, however, particularly mentioned that his
fellow-captives, Dr. Bruce and the editor of the *County
Union*, who were treated as political **prisoners, by** the
compassionate interference of the Inspector **of Prisons,**
were spared this degradation. The district **prison**
was a miserable place. The prisoners were **fed like**
pigs. Bad food and water made them sick, and two
of them died in their cells. Happily, **by the** intervention **of** Mr. **George** Phillippo, the barrister, and the
Baptist missionaries, after a cruel captivity of thirty-
four days, **a writ of Habeas** Corpus was obtained from
Judge Kerr, **and on the** 21st December Mr. Palmer
was released on bail, and ordered to appear before the
Special Commission in Kingston on the 10th February.
To **the last he remained** entirely ignorant of the

charge on which he had been arrested. The Attorney-General was instructed by the Queen's Advocate-General not to disclose it, and it was not until the indictment had been found by the Grand Jury on the day of trial, and the Court had directed a copy of it to be furnished, that the offence was known either to the accused or his counsel. Mr. Palmer was indicted for "seditious language" used at the Court House in Kingston on the 3rd May, at a meeting "held to support the statements of Dr. Underhill's letter." The resolutions and speeches may have contained a little unsound political economy, and some severe reflections on the Government and House of Assembly, but not a word of disloyalty, or that savoured of sedition. On receiving the indictment, the first step taken by counsel was to place on record thirteen pleas touching the legal and constitutional character of the jury itself. After argument and a night's consideration, the Chief Justice pronounced a judgment in favour of Mr. Palmer, and he was discharged.

Notwithstanding this damaging check to the prosecution, the representative of the Crown renewed the indictment. It had been proved that the jury panel was improperly selected by the clerk of the Provost Marshal, and persons omitted from it who it might be supposed would take an unprejudiced view of the cases brought before them. Although the previous decision of the Chief Justice had thrown the gravest doubts on the legal constitution of the jury as empanelled, every effort made by Mr. Phillippo to set

the jury panel aside failed. The counsel for the
Crown persisted in the trial, and on Monday, the 19th
February, Mr. Palmer was a second time arraigned on
an indictment, if not in exactly the same words,
similar in purport to the one previously quashed.

The result was a foregone conclusion. Every ob-
jection was overruled. An eye-witness thus describes
the scene:—" I sat so as to be able to keep an eye on the
jury-box. I observed the utmost eagerness in listen-
ing to the evidence for the prosecution, but as soon
as the defence had begun, most of the jurors became
listless, and, except occasionally, they seemed scarcely
to pay the least attention to the witnesses." The chief
witness, named Fouché, was a man no jury in England
would have believed. He was ignorant of shorthand.
He swore he had made notes of the speeches delivered,
and then enlarged them from memory five months
afterwards. Testimony was given that Mr. Palmer
had never uttered the words attributed to him, yet, on
the evidence of this one man, in about ten minutes
the jury came into Court with a verdict of guilty.
Even the Attorney-General (the prosecutor) made the
damaging admissions: **(1)** That the meeting on the
3rd May was a lawful one, legally convened ; and (2)
that it had no connection with the Morant Bay outbreak. Yet it was not till that event had taken place,
five months afterwards, that the prosecution was
thought of. But the Governor was driven by events
to find a justification for his accusations against
Baptist ministers, and for the atrocious measures employed in the suppression of the so-called rebellion. Mr.

Palmer was therefore included with other persons in an indictment for conspiracy ; but the case broke down so utterly in the hands of the Attorney-General, that on the advice of the Chief Justice this part of the prosecution was abandoned, even before any witnesses had been called.* The Rev. D. J. East, who was present day by day at all these mock trials, writes: " I generally travelled to the Court with the Attorney-General. One morning, while the trials were going on, I said to him, ' Well, Mr. Attorney-General, suppose you get a conviction, what then ? ' ' Oh,' he said, ' twenty-four hours.' No one could have been more surprised than the Government Prosecutor that Mr. Palmer should have been sentenced, not for *twenty-four hours*, but for two months."

At the termination of his imprisonment Mr. Palmer was heartily welcomed by his flock in a warm and eloquent address, at a public meeting held in his chapel on the 19th April. To the end of his days, prolonged some twenty-five years, he retained the esteem and affection of his church, and of all who knew his genuine excellence and devotedness as a minister of Christ.

---

* For fuller details of the events here summarised I must refer to the *Missionary Herald*, for 1866, pp. 13, 21, 37, 58, 89, 137. See also Report of the Royal Commission, p. 304.

CHAPTER XI.

T HE announcement on the 12th December of the supersession of Mr. Eyre by the appointment of Sir Henry Storks, and the resolution of the English Government to make a thorough inquiry into all the circumstances of the outbreak by a Royal Commission, of which Sir H. Storks would be the head, rapidly quieted the agitation in England.

It may be interesting, by a few quotations from my letters to Jamaica, to mark the progress of events as they became known to me.

"*E. B. U. to the Rev. D. J. East.*

"**London,** December 15th.

"Finding my letters intercepted, I have not written the last two mails so fully as I would have done; but now I think we may write freely again. Sir Henry Storks, at all events, will look calmly at the state of affairs, and I do not doubt that the truth will be fully elicited.

"As I expected, Governor Eyre has attempted to fasten on my letter the origin of this lamentable outbreak. His despatch to Mr. Cardwell (of the 20th

October), published here too late for me to notice in my letter of the 16th November, distinctly names me, and implicates a few (who they are he does not say) of our brethren. Of course, the *Times* took up the slander, which I immediately met by writing the editor stating the real facts of the case.

"It has been curious to see the effect. As it became known that Governor Eyre was himself the publisher of my letter, and by the course he took gave it the importance it has acquired, one after another of our public prints vindicated me and expressed astonishment at the absurdity of the charge.* But its effect on the public mind with regard to Governor Eyre himself was most prejudicial. Here, said they, 'is a case in which we have the full means of testing the Governor's judgment and capacity. Dr. Underhill's letter is before us. It is a letter that ought to have been written to a Secretary of State, and is totally incapable of promoting sedition. Yet Governor Eyre attributes to this mild and courteous production all the mischief that has been so dreadfully crushed. Governor Eyre must have acted under panic, or is totally unfit to hold so responsible an office.'

"Then came the account of Gordon's death, and his remarkable letter to his wife, and the almost unanimous judgment of lawyers that he was illegally arrested, tried, and executed. Then were added the details of

---

* From the *Daily News* of Monday, November 20th :—" We published Dr. Underhill's letter last Tuesday, and we believe a more temperate representation of the causes of popular suffering was never made."

the repression, its awful extent and indiscriminating vengeance, lit up with the fiendish glee of the actors. Indeed, I do not remember in my time so deep and profound a feeling of horror as the severities inflicted by the soldiery and the Maroons have produced.

"The Maroon glorification is a shocking business. It has done Governor Eyre much harm in the minds of thoughtful people that he should have employed them, and then given them a roving commission to kill and slay. That dance round the gallows-tree was a dreadful exhibition of savagery. Yet the writer who gives the account of it calls it a 'grand sight.' You cannot then wonder that the mind and heart of England have been roused, and the Government constrained to take measures that will create no little consternation among the agents of this frightful tragedy.

"Of course I have now published (and for the first time) my letter to Mr. Cardwell. I gave no copy of it to anyone either here or in Jamaica. Now my vindication required that it should appear under my own hand. I have added to it some of the resolutions passed at the public meetings in Jamaica, especially your reply to Governor Eyre's circular, schedules and all.* Already about a thousand copies have been sold, and we are sending a copy to every member of both Houses of Parliament. It is felt everywhere to be a complete vindication both of your proceedings

---

* "Dr. Underhill's Letter, and an Explanatory Statement." London : Arthur Miall, Bouverie Street. November 24th, 1865. 8vo.

and mine, and has had its effect in guiding public opinion. *

"I will send you a copy by the mail, as you will like to see my explanatory statement. We had proposed vigorous action with regard to the Bill of Pains and Penalties for Dissent; but, as it has been withdrawn, it will not be necessary to complain to the Government.

"Of the destruction of the Constitution of Jamaica I shall say nothing now. I can hardly imagine that the Colonial Office will allow it to pass without a Parliamentary inquiry. Indeed, this panic-stricken legislation will need to be reviewed altogether when Parliament assembles."

"*E. B. U. to George Phillippo, Esq., Barrister-at-Law.*
"London, December 15th, 1865.

"This mail will convey to Jamaica Sir H. Storks. His first duty will be to supersede Governor Eyre, and then to enter on a thorough investigation of all the circumstances attending the recent most lamentable

---

* The *Saturday Review* spoke of Governor Eyre's attack on me as "extravagant injustice." The *Athenæum* of December 16th: "The general accuracy and honesty of the letter have been sufficiently attested. Dr. Underhill would have been blameworthy had he neglected to put his special information at the service of the country." "S. G. O.," in the *Daily Telegraph*: "I cannot be expected to coincide with Dr. Underhill in all that the letter in question contains; but I do not hesitate to say that it appears to me to be a most temperate and truthful production, and in no way deserving of the anathemas which Governor Eyre hurls against it."

outbreak.   As I write it is not known who the
English Government will appoint as his colleagues ;
but I have every reason to believe men of eminence
will be chosen, to labour with the new Governor in
elucidating the origin of the riot at Morant Bay and
the manner of its repression.   In the despatch of
Governor Eyre to Mr. Cardwell, published in the
London Gazette of the 18th November, Mr. Eyre has
not scrupled to accuse me as the chief cause of the
outbreak.   He names me, while he refers to other
Baptist missionaries, omitting their names.   Of this
portion of the despatch I send you a copy.   In the
judgment of my friends, legal and others, this accusation gives me a *status* before the Commissioners, and
the right to appear and take part in the proceedings
of the Court.

"We do not yet know in what way the Commissioners will proceed ; but can hardly doubt that the
Inquiry will be an open one, and that parties directly
interested will be allowed to appear either in person
or by their representatives.

"The object of my writing you is, therefore, to
request and to authorise you to appear for me before
the Commissioners, to watch the proceedings ; if
necessary also to call witnesses on my behalf, and to
cross-examine others who may give any evidence
bearing on my position in the matter.   If you think
it necessary to have the assistance of a solicitor, or the
etiquette of the profession in Jamaica requires you to
be instructed by a solicitor, you will kindly secure the
services of Mr. Harvey.   His long acquaintance with

the affairs of our Mission will give him advantages no
one else can possess. Besides, I have the pleasure of
personal acquaintance with him.

" You will note that Governor Eyre in his despatch
alludes to a few Baptist missionaries as alike guilty
with me of furthering the rebellion. Who they are I
cannot say. But it has occurred to us here that the
position given me before the Commissioners by
Governor Eyre, actually naming me, may be made use
of to watch the proceedings for them also, and I shall
be glad if you will do this. I dare say some of our
brethren will take care that the Commissioners shall
be informed as to their share in the outbreak ; but you
will greatly add to our obligations to you if you will
aid them in every way in your power to justify themselves from the scandalous accusations of Governor
Eyre."

"E. B. U. to the Rev. B. Millard, of the same date.

" The Jamaica Mail tells us that the Bill of Pains
and Penalties for Dissenters is withdrawn by your
Government, but that another to apply to native
Baptists only is to be substituted for it. To-day we
had a meeting of various dissenting bodies, and have
sent in a resolution to Lord Russell begging him to
direct the Governor to disallow all such Bills. We
intend to oppose every Act that limits religious
liberty. If the native Baptists talk sedition, the
ordinary laws are quite strong enough to punish
them. If such Bills are allowed to pass, a very little
twisting will make them applicable to a wider circle

than they professedly embrace. On principle, every
limitation of religious liberty should be rejected."

The continuance of the "excessive and unlawful
severities" alleged in the Privy Council Minute, rendered it necessary that no time should be lost in
entering on the proposed Inquiry into "the origin,
nature and circumstances" of the disturbances, and
the measures adopted in the course of the suppression.
The "Commission of Inquiry" was resolved upon, and
a draft of the necessary document was approved at
the Privy Council held at Windsor on the 11th of
December. It was declared necessary at once to
suspend Governor Eyre, and not only was Sir Henry
Storks appointed head of the Commission, he was
invested with all necessary powers for the government of the island. But during the sittings of the
Commissioners, Mr. Eyre is directed to remain in
Jamaica. It is obvious that no fair or full inquiry
could be made so long as he was at the head of the
Administration, and the legal representative of the
Crown. Such a position would have opened the way
to every kind of obstruction, and would ensure the
continuance of the acts of injustice that were being
daily perpetrated.

Before the opening of the Commission, and during
the later weeks of his administration, we find Mr. Eyre
busy in passing an Act by which he could absolve
himself from all blame as to the illegal character of
his proceedings; while another Act conferred upon
him the power of imprisonment, without trial, of

persons exposed to arrest for acts committed either during or after the existence of martial law. The arrest of Mr. Sidney Levien, of the *County Union*, as we have seen,* was declared by the Chief Justice to be both illegal and unconstitutional. By another section, the Governor could, at his pleasure, deprive the people of Jamaica of the safeguards still existing against an unnecessary and improper declaration of martial law. By Chapter 5 of the same series of enactments, the forfeiture of the property was directed of all persons pronounced guilty of treason or felony, by the courts-martial that had been held during the time of terror, and the proceeds thereof were to be placed over against extraordinary expenses occasioned by the rebellion. By another Act the severity of the lash for larceny, and other minor offences, was increased. But perhaps the most monstrous and unconstitutional of all these Acts was the one intended to deprive persons accused of seditious offences, committed during martial law, or within six months thereafter, of trial by the civil courts, by handing them over to military tribunals. And finally may be mentioned the offensive and tyrannical Bill for the Regulation of Dissenting Chapels,† by which every Nonconformist chapel might be closed as a nest of sedition.

Happily, these proceedings of the moribund Legislature of Jamaica were never sanctioned by Her

---

* *Ante*, p. 113.

† *See* No. 1 of Jamaica Papers, published by the Jamaica Committee, pp. 60 to 68.

Majesty's Government. But it was made abundantly clear that there was no prospect of better government or of wiser administration under the existing Constitution, or of any effective measures being taken to find a remedy for the grievances and evils out of which the recent disturbances had sprung.

Within six days of the issue of the resolution of the Privy Council, Sir Henry Storks sailed in the *Shannon* for Jamaica, and immediately on his arrival assumed "all the powers of the Crown, both civil and military," which the Queen had conferred upon him, for "the completeness and effectiveness of the Inquiry."* The administration of affairs was vested in his hands during the whole of his stay in the island. His colleagues, Mr. Recorder Russell Gurney and Mr. Recorder Maule, quickly followed.

Sir Henry Storks arrived in Kingston on January 6th, 1866, and the next day took the necessary oaths. Being Sunday, his full inauguration was deferred to the following day. It took place at King's House, Spanish Town, the seat of Government and the Governor's residence, amid the salutes of artillery and the jubilant shouts of the people, who pressed forward to witness the commencement of a new era in the history of Jamaica.

The arrival of the new Governor, at once diffused throughout the island a feeling of confidence and hope, to which the people had long been strangers. He was received with rapturous enthusiasm. The

---

* Mr. Cardwell's Speech at Oxford on the 2nd January.

reign of terror was over, and that of law and order was begun. Loyal men had for many weeks been living in continual peril. After all the vengeance that had been taken, and although the greatest order prevailed throughout the island, men were still trembling for their lives when Sir Henry Storks landed on its shores. No one dared to express an opinion contrary to that prevailing in Government circles. Opinion was terrorised. It was still the fashion to speak of recent events as a "wide-spread rebellion," simmering still in quiet corners, and to be read in the scowling looks of the sufferers. The arrival of the new Governor dispelled these apprehensions, and a truer estimate began to express itself of the nature and extent of the crimes which had been committed, and of the character of the parties engaged in the commission of them.

At their first meeting, on the 20th January, the Royal Commissioners explained their powers and defined the extent of the Inquiry. It would be an open one, "full, searching, and impartial." Witnesses would be summoned who were presumed to be able to give information on the events of the outbreak. Their evidence would be taken on oath. If their evidence criminated any individual, that person would be allowed to test its accuracy, and to tender counter-evidence in reply. The Court would not confine the witnesses to those only who were summoned, but would willingly receive information from others able to throw light on the late transactions.

The Commissioners further expressed their willing-

ness to grant, to certain legal representatives of
parties interested in these proceedings, the privilege
of questioning witnesses, and producing evidence
strictly relative to the Inquiry. Of these, special
mention may be made of John Gorrie, Esq., and
John Horne Payne, Esq., of London, appearing on
behalf of Mr. Gordon and other injured parties, at
the cost of the Jamaica Committee formed for this
purpose in England. Also, George Phillippo, Esq.,
barrister-at-law, of Kingston, who appeared as the
representative of Dr. Underhill and the Baptist missionaries, implicated by Mr. Eyre as parties in the
so-called "rebellion."

The Commissioners, however, considered it their
duty to limit the Inquiry somewhat strictly to the
events which had taken place in St. Thomas-in-
the-East, antecedent and subsequent to the outbreak; so that investigation into the general character of Mr. Eyre's administration, except so far
as it bore upon the actual events of the "rebellion," was ruled as unnecessary. Thus, the general
condition of the island, and the transactions arising out of, and incident to, the publication of
my letter, could be received only as indirectly
illustrating the origin of the outbreak at Morant Bay.
The grave questions of Jamaica government, the condition of the people under the laws in operation,
and the general conduct of Mr. Eyre's administration
were passed by as irrelevant. The term "origin" of
the outbreak, was interpreted as embracing those
events only which related to the riot at Morant Bay.

The "Inquiry," it was stated, found its natural limit in the facts which occurred in the parish where the outbreak took place.

It will subsequently be seen that in this limitation lies the weakness, and partly unsatisfactory character, of the Commissioners' Report. But whatever may be the shortcomings of the Inquiry, as thus cramped and confined, the praise of diligence and unwearied pursuit of their object must at least be fully accorded to the Commissioners. They displayed the most anxious desire, and spared no pains, to discover the truth. They showed an admirable demeanour towards every class of witnesses, to the poor negro as well as to the most exalted personages. Their conduct was marked by patience and a most commendable impartiality. They listened with interest and marked attention to the most illiterate native, and gave the amplest opportunity to every man to state, and even to correct, the information he brought to their knowledge.

It would be impossible and inconsiderate to follow the proceedings of the Commission day by day, for which ample materials exist not only in the well-digested Report of the Commissioners, but also in the letters of the newspaper correspondents to the English journals. The proceedings maintained their interest to the last, and were read by all classes with the greatest avidity. The Report must be received with the heartiest recognition of its excellence, and with admiration of the laborious devotedness of the Commissioners to their task. It is a just and impartial statement of the lamentable events which they had to investigate.

9*

I shall, however, attempt a somewhat extended analysis of the contents of the Report, so as to enable my readers to form their own judgment. It will be seen that this is no light task, when I describe the general characteristics of the voluminous papers before me.

The first part of the Report, some forty pages in length, consists of a condensed narrative of the origin of the disturbances, and of the outbreak itself, and a review of the conduct of the persons engaged in the suppression. The case of Mr. Gordon is examined in much detail, and a few sentences are given to the trials of the political prisoners, who were brought before the courts-martial. Finally, the question of the necessity and duration of martial law is discussed

In conclusion, the Commissioners sum up the result of the whole inquiry. The extent of the slaughter at Morant Bay and its neighbourhood by the rioters, was accurately ascertained to be twenty-two persons in all, white and black; but that the horrible outrages on the dead, so minutely detailed by Governor Eyre, had no existence. On the other hand, the investigation establishes, in the judgment of the Commissioners, the following facts:—That the punishments inflicted on the people were excessive; that the names are known of at least 439 persons who were shot or hung, many of whom were entirely innocent of any crime whatever; that a thousand dwellings were wantonly and cruelly burnt; and that certainly not fewer than six hundred persons, men and women, were scourged in a most reckless manner, those at Bath with the greatest barbarity; besides many of them being sentenced, after flogging, to various terms of imprisonment.*

The second part of the Report consists of the evidence itself. This forms a volume of 1,075 folio pages, with an appendix of 90 pages more. The Inquiry lasted fifty-one days, during which time 730 persons were examined, some of them more than once. The number of questions and answers was 49,158.

The evidence seems to me, however, to justify a far stronger condemnation of the parties engaged in the suppression than the Commissioners have ventured to pronounce. Their language is timid and hesitating when it ought to have been unsparing and firm.

The third part is devoted wholly to the papers laid before the Commissioners by Governor Eyre. It is a volume of 482 pages, and consists of very numerous documents collected by him in vindication of his proceedings, with his comments thereon. Their value is not great, but they illustrate Governor Eyre's weakness of judgment, and his ready belief of every lying rumour that floated to his ears. By the Commissioners these papers were rejected as evidence. In their opinion they were not proofs of the guilt of the parties Mr. Eyre had accused, nor could they be received as a correct account of the causes of those events in which he was the chief actor. They sufficed, however, to show the grounds of the course he pursued.

* Report, p. 40.

CHAPTER XII.

PART I.—THE LAND QUESTION.

THE Commissioners were instructed specially to inquire into "the origin and nature of the disturbances." This portion of their task seems to me to have been very imperfectly accomplished, if regard be had to events antecedent to the outbreak at Morant Bay. Ignoring these, they tell us that the first resistance to "lawful authority" occurred on Saturday, the 7th October; but that it was proved that, two or three weeks before, meetings had been held in the vicinity of Morant Bay, at which an oath was administered and the names of the persons sworn were recorded. The terms of the oath are not shown. Yet one, at least, of the policemen to whom the oath was administered was made to say, "Swear, so help me, God, to tell the truth, and nothing but what was the truth." Another man, a book-keeper, declares that he was asked, "Do you join us?" and then, on answering "Yes," he was told to kiss the Bible. It is clear that the oath, whatever its object, did not reveal any unlawful purpose.

Nevertheless, combining with this the wild statements made by several persons as to what they heard black men say, both before and after the outbreak, the Commissioners conclude that there was on the part of the rioters " a preconcerted plan," and that murder was directly contemplated—a conclusion that the evidence does not sustain, if it be meant that a "plan" existed previous to the Saturday. There was some vague evidence given that drilling was carried on at the meetings referred to; but on this point the Commissioners lay no stress, as it was proved to be a harmless amusement and well known to the authorities. The evidence shows that there was no attempt at organisation. Negroes are incapable of it. They are excitable and impulsive enough ; they may easily be provoked, perhaps, to the extent of a riot; but to combine for general and considered action they display little thought or skill. The alleged "planned resistance to lawful authority" amounted, in fact, to no more than this:—That the events of Saturday forced on their minds the uselessness of all appeals to those to whom, as their judges and masters, they had a right to look for redress, and led them to resolve no longer to submit to the oppression under which they suffered. The riot was, therefore, entirely local in its origin, and sprang from causes which, though in general operation throughout the island, had reached a climax that was intolerable in St. Thomas-in-the-East.

It must be distinctly remembered how short was the time for preparation, and how closely the move-

ment of the people was connected with the perverse
action of the magistrates on the Saturday. There is
positively no evidence at all that any plan had been
formed, or any resolve to resist or commit murder
thought of, previous to that day. Certainly the
Commissioners must have often felt bewildered by the
evidence which was brought before them. They say,
" The negroes were for the most part uneducated
peasants, speaking in accents strange to the ear, often
in a phraseology of their own, with vague conceptions
of number and time, unaccustomed to definiteness or
accuracy of speech, and in many cases still smarting
under a sense of injuries sustained." * Evidence was
drawn from all quarters—from editors and writers in
newspapers ; from the loose talk of the nursery ; from
alarmed magistrates, who heard in every sound of the
estate-horn a summons to the fight. The scared looks
of the frightened peasantry, after they had heard of
the horrors of martial law ; the jokes of friends in
the intercourse of private life ; the absence of people
from the markets ; the vague rumours which accompanied or followed the political meetings ; the
exasperated language of men smarting under fresh
acts of injustice—all were given in as witnessing to
the presence of conspiracy. But proofs of general
or local seditious intention the evidence utterly
fails to establish. The riot was the outburst of
long-endured suffering, and of down-trodden serfs
animated by a common feeling of hatred for their

---

* Report, p. 8.

oppressors. They were united, not as conspirators, but as men similarly wrought upon by common grievances, suddenly crystallised by the destruction of the last hope of redress.*

Of the "manifold" causes which culminated in the riots and atrocities at Morant Bay the Commissioners select only three for special mention. The first was the desire of the disturbers of order to obtain land free from the payment of rent. The evidence on this point was both imperfect and unsatisfactory. It does not appear that the views of the people themselves were ascertained with regard to the tenure on which they held their land. Inquiries were chiefly confined to persons whose interests as proprietors of estates or as landowners were adverse to those of the people. At Stony Gut, near to Morant Bay, a Mr. Anderson claimed to be the owner of certain settlements. Says the Clerk of the Peace, "For seven or eight years past the people have been under the impression that the property belongs to the Crown, and that it is 'Queen's land,' as they call it, and that Mr. Anderson has no right to it." It was one of many cases that may be cited where the freedmen have purchased plots, paid the money to the presumed owner, and have afterwards found the transaction repudiated by some other person, who had subsequently put forward a claim to be the real proprietor.

An illustration or two may be given from the history of affairs at Morant Bay. Mrs. Herschell, whose

---

* See *ante*, pp. 55 to 66.

husband was one of the victims, says that in August the people of their estate at Sunning Hill, which the Rev. Mr. Herschell had lately bought, refused the payment of rent, on the ground that the land was free. But from the evidence of the Bishop of Kingston, it appears that Mr. Herschell was selling off this estate in small lots, and that there were disputes about the boundaries. The Bishop further depicts the character of this clerical landowner, of whose grasping spirit after land he disapproved, in the following words :—" He was of a disputatious, litigious disposition rather, a man who would not let a trifle pass unnoticed when it would have been better to do so." It cannot be wondered at that such a man had excited great animosity against himself. He was one of the first to fall a prey to the rage of the people on the fatal October 11th. And yet the Bishop adds that, as far as he had ever seen the people there, they were " generally a docile and loyal people." * Certainly the Bishop's testimony does away with the notion that people desired the land rent free.

In the evidence of Mr. Skyers, a magistrate of St. George's Parish, we find him declaring that the request of a tenant to have a reduction in his rent really meant, that the Queen had given the people a right to be " rent free and land free "; for which idea, he candidly admitted, he had no foundation in anything the man had said. † He added further that, although a magistrate, he was not aware of

---

° Report, p. 778.   † *Ibid*, p. 592.

any conspiracy or combination, secret or otherwise, to employ force to change the established order of things.

Attorney - General Heslop informs us that Mr. Hire, who was killed by the rioters, was involved in numerous disputes with the people about their rights to the land they occupied. Many of them had been summoned to the Circuit Court. Mr. Hire wanted "to run his lines" through their grounds; that is, to fix the boundaries of the property in dispute; but he could not do it owing to the resistance he encountered. To meet such cases, the Legislature had passed an Act to empower persons to run a surveyor's line through the property claimed by poor people, without their consent. Mr. Hire had no right to entitle him to take the course he did, and for which he was remonstrated with by the Attorney-General himself. *

Many disputes arose out of the desire of the people to occupy outlying and uncultivated lands on the borders of the estates; but the Attorney-General declared emphatically that he had never heard that there had been any agitation arising out of claims to occupy them without the payment of rent. No evidence was adduced that the people wished or attempted by force to take possession of these lands; they were often selfishly refused the occupation, although willing to pay rent for them.

There is one notable case reported by the Commis-

---

* Report, p. 330.

sioners, that of a Mr. Gyles, who possessed some uncultivated land especially suitable for the growth of
provisions. "The people," Mr. Gyles said, "made
several applications to rent this land, and I refused
renting it." Following on this, he said that the people
told him that the Queen had given it to them. The
question was put: "What was the particular nature
of the application, and the nature of their remarks
about the Queen?" Answer: "They came to ask me
if I would rent them some of my land, and I refused
doing it. They said the Queen would give it." Now
here is a man possessing good provision land essential
for the livelihood of the negro. It is lying unused.
Again and again on his own showing they make
application to rent it. He won't. Can we wonder
that poor, uneducated, starving people catch at any
hope, at any rumour, that such an unnatural and
wicked state of things must be altered? Have these
famished men and women no right to live—no claim
on such an owner for the necessaries of existence? *

During the sittings of the Commission an event
occurred which gave the Commissioners a striking
example of this cause of the disturbances. It took
place at the Hartlands, a settlement about five miles
from Spanish Town. The estate once belonged to a
merchant of the name of Hart, and comprised about
2,500 acres. Shortly after the abolition of slavery
portions of this land, in an uncultivated state, were
purchased by people principally from the neighbour-

---

* Report, p. 459.

ing estates. Some paid for their allotments at once, and received their titles; others paid by instalments, and had only their receipts to show for their legal occupation. At Mr. Hart's death, his affairs fell into confusion, and for twenty years scarcely any attention was given to the property. Trespassers were said to have taken possession of the unsold portions. At length the people generally were called upon to show their titles, but in 1862 a fire in Kingston destroyed a large proportion of the papers the peasantry had sent in. The rights of the several owners were thus thrown into great uncertainty and confusion. Measures were taken, at the instigation of partisans of Ex-Governor Eyre, that threatened another carnival of blood, and Mr. Eyre immediately availed himself of this incident to justify his proceedings at Morant Bay.

By the providential interference of the Rev. J. M. Phillippo, Baptist minister at Spanish Town, and with the full approbation of Sir Henry Storks, the catastrophe was at the last moment averted; and by the wise and conciliatory action of Sir Henry Storks and his eminent successor, Sir John Peter Grant, the questions in dispute were finally settled by arbitration. For his active and successful exertions, Mr. Phillippo received the "cordial thanks" of the Government. The people were induced voluntarily to obey the laws, and that without the exhibition of any force on the part of the authorities. It cannot be doubted that if Mr. Eyre had adopted a similar course at Morant Bay, which it was quite open to him to do, the nation, and Jamaica itself, would have been spared the tale of horror which history now records.*

PART II.—THE MAGISTRACY.

As the second incentive to the violation of the law, the Commissioners report † "the **want of** confidence generally felt by the labouring class in **the** tribunals, before which most of the disputes affecting their interests were carried for adjudication."

This "**want of** confidence" the Commissioners evidently think was justified. For, in the explanation given in another part of this Report, they say:—"The magistrates are principally **planters and** persons connected with the management **of the** estates. Those who are not so connected are for the most part engaged in business, and their attendance is very irregular. The consequence is, that disputes between employers and labourers, and questions relating to the occupation of land, which are decided in the first instance at Petty Sessions, are adjudicated upon by those whose interests and feelings are supposed to be hostile to the labourer and the occupier." They conclude, "that the difficulties in the way of seeking relief by law were very great, and it was not to be expected that, constituted as the Bench of Magistrates

---

* The story of the Hartlands affair may be read in full in my "Life of the Rev. J. M. Phillippo" (London, 1881). For Mr. Eyre's conduct in the matter, see his letter of the 6th April, 1866, to Sir Henry Storks: Parliamentary Papers, p. 312.

† Report, p. 40.

at present is, it would have the confidence of the labourers." *

The evidence is conclusive on this point. The Petty Sessions Courts were presided over by partial judges. Their sentences were often marked by great severity on the labouring classes and small settlers, and lenient upon the higher. The costs inflicted were extravagant, creating a barrier in the way of redress insurmountable by the poor. The most vexatious delays were interposed by the magistrates themselves, especially when a case against their own class was brought before them for adjudication. Whatever vice can attach to the administration of justice, was found to be existent in these courts, and, of all parishes in the island, St. Thomas-in-the-East stood pre-eminent as the worst.

The origin and concomitants of the riot at Morant Bay clearly show how closely this failure to do justice lay at the foundation of the murderous outbreak which took place. The first symptom of disturbance, as we have seen, began in a Saturday Sessions Court, with a refusal to pay the exorbitant costs exacted in the case of an assault by a boy on a girl. It occasioned a suspension of the business of the Court. The man who told the boy not to pay the costs, but to appeal against the decision, was "shoved" out of Court by the police, and, when arrested for the disturbance that ensued, was rescued by the people present. Out of this rescue came the

* Report, pp. 17, 18.

issue of the twenty-nine warrants against some of the
men engaged in the row, which led directly to the
lamentable events of the following Tuesday and
Wednesday.

Another case tried on the same Saturday was
one of trespass. This arose, say the Commissioners,
" out of a dispute relating to an estate in the neighbourhood of Stony Gut, a portion of which had been
leased out to small occupiers." * This affair, from
the interest felt in it, had caused a numerous
attendance. The question was decided against the
occupiers. There is no doubt that the people, rightly
or wrongly, regarded themselves as unjustly treated,
and, judging by the constitution of the Court, it may
be believed that the people were not altogether
wrong in their contention. The man Miller was convicted, but appealed against the conviction to a
higher court. Alas! he did not live to explain to the
Commissioners the real state of the matter, for he
was put to death at Morant Bay, on the 23rd October,
charged with rebellion. His case was carried to the
Highest Tribunal of all.†

The evidence presents us with a most instructive,
but distressing, picture of this ill-fated parish. The
Hon. Mr. Justice Kerr declares that " St. Thomas-in-
the-East has been conspicuous in Jamaica as a district
torn by dissensions of every kind. It is almost a distress to travel through it. All the leading parties
there, so far back as my recollection extends, rank

---

* Report, p. 11.   † *Ibid.*, p. 1136.

upon one side or the other—two parties, whose spirit towards one another is something which I would rather not speak about. It is very much the reverse of that which should bo expected of Christian men; that is the explanation. I believe, I cannot say I know, but I believe it is a fact of notoriety that Mr. Jackson and his brother justices were in a state of constant dispute; I believe even on the Bench." " I am bound to say that I have come to the conclusion that the labourers of St. Thomas-in-the-East have not that confidence in the administration of justice at Petty Sessions which it is of so much importance to the peace and order of the community they should have." Mr. Justice Kerr further stated that one ground of his unfavourable judgment was the number of appeals that came from the parish.*

Yes, "that is the explanation" of the outbreak. The people were goaded to resistance by the unjust doings and bitter contentions of the magistrates themselves. The honourable Judge might well say their conduct was "the reverse of that which should be expected of Christian men." Among these quarrelsome and partial administrators of the law were two clergymen—Mr. Herschell, who was killed by the rioters, and the Rector, Mr. Cooke, who narrowly escaped with his life.

The character of the magistrates has so important a bearing on the cause of the riot, that I may be permitted to trouble my readers with some further

---

* Report, p. 285.

extracts from the evidence **on this** point. **Mr. J. G.**
Sawkins is the local director **of** the Geological **Sur-**
vey. He **tells us that he had** personal knowledge
of almost **every magistrate in the** parish, and of the
peasantry **as well. He knew well the** Baron **von**
Ketelhodt, and also Mr. **G. W. Gordon.** His examination was **as** follows :—

" Could you judge from your **own** experience and
observation what the state of public **feeling was in**
the parish about the middle of last year ?—I could.

" What did you conclude was the state **of public
feeling** in the **middle** of 1865 ?—A very excited
one.

" **Do you mean disaffected, or only** generally con-
tentious with **regard to election** of members ?—
Personal contention.

" **About** what **subject ?—They** were quarrelling
among themselves almost on **every point.**

" **Public, personal, or private ?—Public as** well as
private.

" Upon public subjects ?—Yes.

" Did **you notice** anything **in** the demeanour **of** the
labouring class **at large** ?—I am speaking now of the
magistrates.

" They were all squabbling, were **they ?—They** were
all squabbling.

" About public **and** personal matters ?—Yes.

" **Did that** extend throughout the whole body of
magistrates ?—**It appeared to be very** general from all
I could understand.

" **Did you gather from** your intercourse with the

magistrates what were the political subjects that agitated them, and made them quarrel among each other?—Some had rendered themselves obnoxious to the others, and they would not sit on the Bench with each other.

"They did not say on what ground they were obnoxious?—I did not gather particulars.

"Only you heard one man abuse his neighbour?—Yes.

"And he returned the compliment back again in the usual way of squabbling?—Yes."

And then Mr. Sawkins goes on to give an illustration in the case of Mr. Hire, who fell a victim in the riot. Between him and Mr. Shortridge the bitterest personal hostility existed, which interfered, on one occasion, in Mr. Sawkins' presence, with the due administration of justice.*

Important evidence on this subject was also given by Mr. T. W. Jackson. He had been twenty-nine years resident in the island as a stipendiary magistrate, and was generally esteemed by the people as just in his conduct on the Bench. He was sent into St. Thomas-in-the-East by Mr. Eyre, in 1860, but was removed on account of his differences with the Custos, Baron von Ketelhodt and on his complaint to Mr. Eyre, in August, 1865. He testifies that, to his knowledge, the people "were most assuredly" dissatisfied with the administration in the parish. Five-sixths of the magistracy were planters, or connected with the

* Report, p. 524.

10*

management of estates; the other sixth were
merchants or shop-keepers. He usually attended
at the Sessions Court in Morant Bay, but there were
constantly dissensions among his colleagues, and he
was generally outvoted by them. There were many
instances of the bias that animated them, and of their
unjust decisions. He gives the following instance :—
" A woman was going to work on an estate. By acci-
dent, apparently, her hoe struck the horse's nose. The
magistrate retorted upon her by supple-jacking her
very severely. She took out a summons against him,
and it came into Court—Court after Court, for about
three months or more ; and it was not until a representation was made to the Governor that a Court could be
formed to try this magistrate up in that district." He
was fined five shillings and costs. Next Court, this
same magistrate tried a case for assault—a trifle com-
pared with the assault he himself had committed—and
he imposed a fine of thirty shillings. This man was one
of the magistrates killed by the rioters at Morant Bay
on the fatal 11th October. In another case, this same
magistrate literally stole a dog from a boy who would
not sell it to him. The boy repossessed himself of
the dog, and the thieving magistrate actually put the
boy in prison for stealing his own dog, and he lay
there untried for two months. No punishment for
this outrage was inflicted. Mr. Jackson's departure
from the district was greatly regretted. It appeared
to the people as if the last ray of hope for impartial
justice was extinguished.*

With such courts and magistrates as these, performing deeds of wrong, and abusing their power in forms so gross and wicked, it is no wonder that we come upon traces of local efforts among the people to set up a jurisdiction for themselves, in which truth and justice might have fair play. A magistrate, Mr. W. C. Miller, of the Parish of St. Thomas, tells us that the people hold "courts of their own in the interior districts of Manchioneal, and punish offences by money fines; and the same procedure had been carried on in the Blue Mountain Valley, at a village called Huntley, up to the time of the rebellion." "I have a summons, now," he said, "that was taken from one of my Africans, since the rebellion, and signed John Lamont, J.P. This man is a field labourer on Serge Island estate." It is dated February 28th, 1865, and as if to show that it was no treasonable attempt to interfere with the lawful rights of the Crown, it is issued in the name of "our Sovereign Lady the Queen," the offence being charged as "against her crown and dignity."*

The truth is, justice was a scarce commodity in the Parish of St. Thomas-in-the-East. The administration of the law was corrupt and oppressive. The magistrates were partisans, covering each other's delinquencies, and refusing justice where their own interests or passions were concerned. The people, with reason, had no confidence in the regular tribunals. It is a wonder that they should have borne for so many years the iniquities to which they were subjected. The Com-

---

* Report, p. 919.

missioners say that when the day of " resistance " came,
it was "against lawful authority." If technically the
authority of the magistrates of St. Thomas-in-the-East
was "lawful," yet was their conduct often stamped
with all the characteristics of illegality, oppression,
and wrong. It is a question not here to be discussed,
but which irresistibly arises to one's lips, whether a
time may not come when resistance to such "authority"
may not be both a virtue and a right. , At all events,
let the poor people of St. Thomas-in-the-East have the
benefit of whatever extenuation such facts as the above
may fairly suggest for the crimes of the 11th October.
If they sinned, they were also sinned against. Their
offences ought in truth to be measured by the wrongs
they endured. Is there no reality in the saying of the
Lord Jesus, " With what measure ye mete, it shall be
measured unto you "?

PART III.—THE UNIVERSAL DISCONTENT.

While the Parish of St. Thomas-in-the-East stood
pre-eminent for misgovernment, the evidence also
establishes the fact that the proceedings of the
Petty Sessions Courts throughout the island were
regarded with extreme dissatisfaction. Some magistrates indeed were forward to affirm, that complainants
in their Courts were well satisfied with their decisions.
But in this matter the magistrates are judges in their
own cause. We have the thoroughly impartial, as
well as judicial, opinions of the highest legal authori-

ties in the island, which put beyond question the unsatisfactory character of "justices' justice," and its heavy cost to the suitors.

Sir Bryan Edwards, the Lord Chief Justice, was asked " Whether there is confidence in the administration of justice by the magistrates of the island?" He tenderly replies, "To a certain extent I think there is not." The connection of the magistracy with the planting interest, "induces a suspicion beyond all question, and to some extent this suspicion may be correct." He goes so far as to state that he has no doubt that this suspicion is justified, even "though there may be perfect honesty of intention among the magistrates." So true is it, that self-interest may blind even good men to their shortcomings.

Sir Bryan Edwards next calls attention to the state of the law with regard to the trespassing of cattle. This is a very serious grievance to the poor peasant. "I have no doubt," he says, "it creates a great deal of dissatisfaction and is often a great hardship. It seems to act most unjustly and injuriously." He then mentions a case among the papers sent to him by the then Governor. "I read them, and pointed out to the Governor the extreme hardship suffered by these persons, whose lands were so much exposed, and who could rarely get redress. Unless a man could say he had sustained damage to the amount of more than forty shillings, it would almost ruin him." It is a well-known fact that the planters seldom enclose their lands, and, as a consequence, their cattle are continually trespassing on the provision grounds of their peasant neighbours. The Chief Justice affirms that practically, in such cases, there is no redress, or only a ruinous one. In fact, both the law and its ministers, in this matter, inflict great injuries on the poor. It would, he said, be an advantage if there were more stipendiary magistrates, who were without any personal connection with the island.[*]

The Honourable **Mr.** Justice Allan **Kerr** also gave evidence on this point, and it brought upon him unmeasured obloquy **in the** island press. We have already seen his **views on** the character of the magistracy of St. Thomas-in-the-East. The evidence now epitomised relates to the entire island. In answer to the Commissioners, he frankly says: " I must say that I believe the law of labourer and employer is altogether in a most unsatisfactory position in Jamaica. I have lived in four of the West India Islands, and in none have I found it so unsatisfactory as here." " In what respect ?" he is asked. He replies, " In this respect: that from the expense to which the parties are put, and from other causes to which I will refer, legal redress is absolutely shut out from one class altogether." " You refer to the labouring class rather than to any other ?" " Yes."

This evidence contrasts strangely with Mr. Eyre's very confident assertion in his despatch of October 20th: " I know of no general grievance under which the negroes of this Colony labour; the same laws as to the administration of justice apply to them as to the white

---

* Report, p. 834.

and coloured inhabitants alike." The Governor's ignorance is fairly astounding.

Judge Kerr next proceeds to indicate the costs which have to be paid before even a case can be brought into Court. He states that the costs are extravagantly high, and the difficulties that a poor suitor has to surmount are both intricate and well-nigh insuperable. He gives the following as an example:—

"It occurred at the end of October, in the year before last. An appeal came before me in which the appellant sought to reverse the judgment of the Court below, which was a judgment against him by default, for not appearing to answer a civil claim. I think a man had sued him for some twelve or fourteen shillings. I called upon the appellant to explain. The statement he made was this: That he lived fifteen miles off. He came to Port Antonio on the Court day, and found no Court sitting. He remained a greater part of the day and then went away. He attended at the next adjourned Court; there was no sitting then. A labouring man's time was valuable. He waited the greater part of the day, and then wheeled about as on the first occasion. He came up the third time; still no Court. He said, 'Is it of any use for me to go up again?' And he allowed the case to go by default." The hardship of such a case is intensified by the badness of the roads, by the entire absence of any public conveyance, and at certain seasons by the severity of the weather. And when the case gets into Court, it not infrequently happens that, for the most trivial reasons, the magistrates will again postpone its consideration.

But the law of appeal is itself most perplexing. "Instead of providing facilities to the complainant for bringing his case to the notice of the Circuit Judge, it is surrounded with snares and formalities and technicalities, which really in the great majority of cases, as I have seen over and over again, render the law of appeal not at all an available opportunity or means of redress." To this Mr. Justice Kerr adds, that in some parishes there is no available lawyer, and the suitor may have to go, perhaps sixty miles, as in a case he mentions, to find an attorney to draw up the requisite papers. No wonder that great dissatisfaction was the consequence of such a denial of justice.

But the Judge is not less decisive and emphatic when speaking of the administration of the law. Here are his well-considered words : "I think it right to state, that I have for years past come to the conclusion, that the present system of the unpaid magistracy in Jamaica is the most unsatisfactory that could well be conceived. Of the two hundred and seventy magistrates that hold the commission of the peace, from personal observation and knowledge of a good many, I should say that more than half were utterly unfit to hold that trust ; unfit by want of education, capacity, social position, and pecuniary independence." He further illustrates the style of legislation in Jamaica by telling us that the Act establishing the above oppressive system of appeal, and which increased the expenses of a suit from 20 to 100 per cent., passed the Legislature without a dissentient voice. The House of Assembly, the presumed popular branch of the Legislature, has never shown itself backward, by insidious laws, to injure the poor and to oppress the labouring class.

Mr. Justice Kerr's opinion on the cause of the disturbances deserves the highest respect, and ought to have weighed with the Commissioners more than it seems to have done, when forming their judgment on the guilt of the rioters :—

"I have no doubt whatever, I think I ought to mention (it is for the Commissioners to consider whether they think it worthy of being noted), that I believe the disaffection of certain parties was caused by the bad administration of justice in the first instance, and to another cause, namely, to the diminished respect for all manner of authority—executive authority, judicial authority, ecclesiastical authority —produced by the turbulent tone of the House of Assembly, and the seditious tone of the public press. I believe these to have been the causes of the melancholy events that are now being inquired into." *

From Judge Kerr's evidence it is clear that nearly all parts of the judicial machinery of the island were equally bad, and productive of cruel wrong. He complains of the utter unfitness of the juries. Nothing was more notorious than the wilfully unjust verdicts they gave. There was much complaint of the manner in which the clerks of the peace fulfilled

---

* Report, pp. 284, 287.

their duties, which indeed were often discharged by incompetent deputies. With these circumstantial and unimpeachable statements in our hands, there is no need to revert to Mr. Eyre's theory of a " diabolical conspiracy," or the action of " wicked agitators and sedition-mongers," to account for the universal dissatisfaction prevailing throughout the island, or for the display of it which the publication of my letter called forth. The testimony confirms and establishes the fact that the negro part of the population had many just causes for their unrest and discontent, and sufficiently explains the origin of those " feelings of hostility towards political and personal opponents " which animated, in the opinion of the Commissioners, the minds of the men who committed the crimes of Morant Bay.

I may here close my examination of the Report with regard to the origin and nature of the causes from which the disturbances sprang. I cannot but think that my readers will be fully convinced of the truth of the averments of my letter, and that the communication to Mr. Cardwell of the facts as I knew them was fully justified. It is clearly with some hesitation that, in his latest justificatory letter to Mr. Cardwell, Mr. Eyre very anxiously explains that he did not publish the letter he incriminates, and was therefore not responsible for the effects he affirms that it produced. But just as clearly the Commissioners did not believe this pet fancy of Mr. Eyre's, for they refused every attempt made by the representation of the missionaries and Dr. Underhill to bring the facts of the case before them. In truth, by the interpretation put upon the text of the Commission, the Inquiry failed to elicit, or to deal with, many important events bearing on the origin and nature of the disturbances. I cannot but think that had the investigations of the Royal Commissioners taken a more extended range, on the one hand less prominence would have been given to the errors of Mr. Gordon, and the crimes of the negroes; and, on the other, much stronger relief would have been given to the acts of oppression and injustice suffered from the time of emancipation by the people, the lawlessness of the magistrates, and the general mal-administration of affairs, which provoked the people to resistance, and created throughout the island deep discontent, and a spirit of bitter resentment against the authorities, which the evidence, as it stands, shows to have been fully justified.

CHAPTER XIII.

IN the Report of the Royal Commissioners it may be noted with some surprise that there is no deliverance on the conduct of the Baptist missionaries.* In "the nefarious proceedings" which took place in the island subsequent to the publication of my letter, Mr. Eyre distinctly names as having taken part in them "a few Baptist missionaries, who, like Messrs. Henderson, Reid, Dendy, Hewett, and Maxwell, endorse, at public meetings or otherwise, all the untruthful statements or inuendoes propagated in Dr. Underhill's letter." Not that *all* the missionaries were involved in the offence; for he adds : " Whilst it is my duty to point out how mischievous has been the influence of a few of the Baptist ministers and of various members of that persuasion, it is equally my duty, and a pleasure to me, to state that I believe a large majority of the Baptist ministers have been most anxious to support the authorities, to teach their people to be loyal and industrious, and to endorse the advice given to the peasantry by Her Most Gracious Majesty."

Why the five ministers named were singled out by

---

* Blue Book : Return, June 26th, 1866, p. 13, &c.

the Governor for reproach and blame, and their conduct contrasted with that of the majority of their
colleagues, may afterwards appear; but it is remarkable that the Royal Commissioners should, in this
respect, entirely omit all reference to them or to the
author of the incriminated letter. Among the causes
to which they ascribe the disturbances at Morant
Bay, and into the origin of which it was their duty to
inquire, "the nefarious proceedings" of these Baptist
missionaries find no place. As we have seen, the
Royal Commissioners trace to three chief causes, or
rather grievances, the people's resistance to lawful
authority:—(1) The desire to obtain land free of
rent; (2) want of confidence in the administration of
justice; and (3) hostility to the white inhabitants,
especially to their political opponents. But the Commissioners entirely disregard the accusations brought
by Mr. Eyre against these "few Baptist missionaries."

This singular omission finds its explanation in a
correspondence (appended to the Report) between the
Royal Commissioners and certain of the missionaries.
On the 26th January, 1866—that is, on the second
day after the Commission commenced the reception
of evidence—the Rev. J. M. Phillippo, of Spanish
Town, the senior missionary on the spot, brought the
subject to their notice, and afterwards, on the 26th of
February, in order to obtain a written reply from the
Commissioners, forwarded to them, on behalf of the
ministers, a memorial, signifying "their desire and
ability to vindicate Dr. Underhill and themselves"
from the charges, expressed or implied, of having

been accessory by their letters and meetings, as also in other ways, to the late riot at Morant Bay, and the chief authors of the dissatisfaction that is stated to have existed in other parts of the country."* The memorial was signed by the Revs. J. M. Phillippo, W. Dendy, J. E. Henderson, B. Millard, and D. J. East, all of them long residents in Jamaica, men of standing, and held in great respect throughout the island. Both in private, as well as in open Court, the desire of the ministers was urged upon the Commission.

The reply was courteous, but decided. The request could not be entertained, and that on the following grounds :—" No evidence (it was stated) has been given before the Commissioners affecting the character of Baptist missionaries in relation to the recent disturbances in St. Thomas-in-the-East, to which subject their Inquiry is limited." And in regard to Dr. Underhill, " the form of attack was so modified as to enable the Commissioners on the same grounds to disallow any evidence in refutation."

His Excellency Sir H. Storks and his colleagues were, therefore, of opinion " that it would be a departure from the rule laid down by the Commissioners to admit evidence in contradiction of charges of which they have no cognisance."

Two things are clear from this reply: first, that Ex-Governor Eyre did not dare, or did not think it prudent, to repeat the accusations of his despatches

* Appendix to Report, p. 1160.

before the Commissioners; and second, that in the judgment of the Commissioners the cause alleged by Mr. Eyre as originating the riot was no cause at all; for it was their special duty, the very object of their Inquiry, to ascertain "the origin, nature, and circumstances of the said disturbances." If the Baptist missionaries and Dr. Underhill, or any of them, had contributed in the remotest degree to the outbreak at Morant Bay, the Commissioners were surely bound not to wait for Mr. Eyre to restate his charges, or for the accused missionaries to bring them to their notice. They should of their own motion have diligently sought out the facts. The missionaries, by appearing before the Court in person, as well as by writing and by their counsel, George Phillippo, Esq., challenged the accuser; they offered every facility for pursuing the inquiry, and they importunately pressed for an investigation. They omitted no possible course open to them to bring to the test of the closest scrutiny what they had done and said. But their accuser did not venture to repeat his untrue allegations, and the Commissioners ruled that the question was therefore beyond their cognisance.

In the ex-Governor's second and final examination, he declared that he had no charges to bring against the Baptist missionaries, except one in connection with the "Underhill Meeting" held at Montego Bay, and that he held the majority of the Baptist ministers in high esteem. On this, one of the ministers who took part in that meeting, wrote to the Commissioners claiming to be heard in self-defence. In reply, the

11

Commissioners again explained to counsel that the documents put in by Mr. Eyre, in the course of his examination, were admitted, not as evidence of the "facts" contained in them, but merely as information, whether correct or incorrect, on which Mr. Eyre and his Council acted. So the reports of the speeches made at these "Underhill Meetings" were to be received, not as evidence of the language actually used, or of the effect, whether good or bad, produced by them, but simply as an element which at that time contributed to influence the action of the Island Government. The issue was entirely irrespective of the accuracy of the "facts," and, consequently, the occasion for evidence in explanation or contradiction did not arise.

We are, however, entitled to conclude that, in the judgment of the Commissioners, the Morant Bay riot can have had no part of its origin in the conduct of the accused missionaries, or of the author of the letter. Mr. Eyre's charges were calumnious and in truth groundless, and the course he pursued towards these ministers of the Gospel was dishonourable and unjust.

It is beyond question that it was the sincere desire of the Home Government and of the Royal Commissioners to get at the truth. But, while they in effect exonerated the missionaries, the course taken deprived the parties accused of a public opportunity of vindicating themselves in the most effective manner, from the injurious imputations so abundantly strewed over the pages of the Governor's despatches. His charges and misrepresentations had obtained a world-wide circulation—in Jamaica, in the English Press, and in the voluminous papers published for the information of Parliament. It was but due to these maligned individuals that there should be given a fair opportunity to vindicate their characters from the aspersions so persistently made by Mr. Eyre. It was denied them, and if we now pursue the inquiry, it will have the incidental advantage of throwing further light on the conduct of the Government of Jamaica, to whose misrule the disturbances must in the last resort be attributed.

The first despatch of Mr. Eyre to the Colonial Office, having reference to my letter, is dated the 2nd March, 1865. In acknowledging the receipt of it from Mr. Cardwell, he expresses the opinion that, while there is a considerable amount of distress among all classes in Jamaica, the letter contains "a very exaggerated view of the state of the Colony"; and that, although there is an undoubted increase of the crime of larceny, it does not follow "that the resort to thieving is because the people are starving."

I have already spoken of the intense excitement arising from the "Underhill Meetings,"* and from the bitter discussions in the newspapers which immediately followed the publication of the letter, and of the steps taken by the Governor to obtain information for Mr. Cardwell. From Mr. Eyre's despatch of the 19th April,† it is clear that he did not anticipate any

* See Chapters II. and IV.
† Papers, &c., p. 29, No. 90.

11*

mischievous results from its circulation. While he
combats some of its statements, he deals fairly with it.
There is no trace of a suspicion that Baptist ministers
were or had been engaged in any "nefarious proceedings," occupied as they were in gathering materials
for a reply to the circular requesting their views on
the questions which the letter had raised. It is in
his despatch of the 25th April * that the Governor for
the first time expresses his fears of coming mischief.
He is forwarding the petition to the Queen of certain
poor people of St. Ann's. "This," he says, "is the
first-fruits of Dr. Underhill's letter. I fear the result
will have a very prejudicial influence in unsettling
the minds of the peasantry, making them discontented with their lot, and disinclined to conform to
the laws which regulate their taxation, their civil
tribunals, or their political status—all of which they
have been informed are unjust, partial, or oppressive."

Mr. Eyre was altogether mistaken in supposing that
the St. Ann's petition was the "first-fruits of Dr.
Underhill's letter." It is in evidence that the petition
originated some two or three weeks before the letter
was published, and that no Baptist minister had anything to do with it. Mr. Eyre, in a despatch devoted
to the defence of himself at a later period, endeavours
very evasively to escape from the error into which he
had fallen. He attributed to the letter an influence
which at that time it did not enjoy. It is, however,
probable that Mr. Eyre soon thereafter began to

---

* Papers, &c., p. 135, No. 117.

perceive how unwisely he had chosen his course.
The first of the " Underhill Meetings" took place at
Savanna-la-Mar, on the 21st of April, and there was
the prospect of others to come. Still, up to this
point he had no complaint against the letter or the
missionaries.

On the 6th of May * Mr. Eyre transmitted to Mr.
Cardwell, with other communications, the reply of
the Baptist missionaries to his circular. He very
fairly points out, in his despatch, the differences of
opinion existent among them on two or three of the
subjects touched upon, but says, " The Baptist Society
Report is a very carefully and ably got up paper, and
contains much interesting and valuable information."
And again, " As a whole the Report is a very fair and
candid one, and will convey to Her Majesty's Government much important and useful information." There
is very little criticism in this despatch to which exception can be taken, and the Governor seems at the
time to have had no idea that Baptist missionaries
were disposed to originate, or to join in any " nefarious
proceedings" to create, discontent or disaffection. He
somewhat ungraciously, however, hints that the
falling off of the contributions of their people on
account of their increasing poverty may, " in part, be
due to a growing irreligion, or to an indisposition to
support their ministers."

In the month of May several important " Underhill
Meetings" were held. Mr. Eyre's fears grew with

---

* Papers, &c., p. 139, No. 128.

their progress. The first took place at Kingston, on the 3rd May, at which was present the Rev. E. Palmer, the only Baptist minister there connected with the Missionary Society. Mr. Eyre characterises the meeting as having for its object to induce the descendants of Africa throughout the island " to co-operate for the purpose of setting forth their grievances." It was not till nearly six months had elapsed that Mr. Eyre discovered that this object was seditious, and laid Mr. Palmer open to the charge of conspiracy. Not till the Governor had a purpose to serve in justifying the severities inflicted in St. Thomas-in-the-East, was Mr. Palmer's presence at this meeting deemed a criminal act worthy of punishment.

But the meeting at Montego Bay, on the 19th May, was the first in which Mr. Eyre discerned the evil designs of the Baptist missionaries. Reporting to Mr. Cardwell the resolutions that were passed, he says :— " The meeting appears to have been an amalgamation (for political purposes) between a portion of the country party, who are opposed to the present Executive Committee, and a portion of the Baptist ministers, who desire to back up Dr. Underhill." *

The " mischievous designs " of this meeting were said to be two : the first, to obtain an alteration of the Constitution ; and the second, the annihilation of the Established Church. Strange to say, Governor Eyre's despatches abundantly prove that he was himself an advocate of the abrogation of the Constitution. He

* Papers relative to the Affairs of Jamaica, p. 197, No. 137.

seized the time of panic, in the following October, to induce the Legislature of the island to "immolate itself on the altar of patriotism." And with regard to the Church Establishment, Mr. Eyre has left on record his opinion, in his despatches to the Secretary of State, that its cost is "large in proportion to the revenue," and that its existence is "at variance with the principles, or system, which prevail in the more recently formed colonies." *

Again and again in his despatches does Mr. Eyre refer to the speeches of the missionaries who took part in these meetings. In uniting with others to condemn, in a lawful and constitutional manner, the misrule which was hastening the island to ruin, they committed, in his judgment, an unpardonable offence. From this time must be dated the manifestation of that malevolent spirit with which Dr. Underhill and these ministers were pursued by the Governor and by his partisans, and which culminated in the extravagant charge of their being, with others, the authors of a "wicked and unprovoked rebellion."

I have elsewhere spoken of the placard issued as a reply to the petition from St. Ann's, entitled "The Queen's Advice," and of the refusal of the Baptist ministers generally to assist in its promulgation.† As ministers of religion they were not alone in regarding its circulation as unwise and mischievous. The Rector of Vere, the Rev. J. Garrett, thus wrote to Mr. Eyre:—"I thought it desirable to refrain from

---

* Papers, &c., p. 216.　　　† See *ante*, pp. 24—27.

distributing copies of the Hon. Mr. Cardwell's letter, sent to me by the **Government** for that purpose. In the **then** state **of feeling,** I felt convinced they (the people) would be **rather exasperated** than appeased."

The Rev. H. **Clarke, Curate of** Westmoreland, expresses **his** opinion **more** boldly:—"I don't consider that His Excellency Governor Eyre and his advisers are free from the guilt of inciting to rebellion. They have persistently ignored the distress which everywhere exists among **the** labourers, **and, in** publishing **that most inappropriate reply of** Mr. Cardwell, they **mocked the cry of the poor, and** showed themselves **the mere partisans of** the class opposed to the negroes. **I was as much** filled with amazement **at the recklessness of the Government as with** uneasiness at the **probable consequences of their act, and I** determined **to suppress the placard as far** as **I could in** this neighbourhood."

Events justified the foresight of these ministers and clergymen, **for no act of** Mr. Eyre's Government during the excitement **of the** summer months created greater heart-burning than **this** foolish and **ungracious** proclamation. Yet the Baptist **missionaries,** for their **manly and** courteous **protest, were** insulted by Mr. **Eyre in the correspondence** that ensued, and afterwards **held up as** guilty **participators** in the disturbances **which** incompetence and injustice had produced.

Next we read in a despatch, dated July 24th, that the **disorder now apprehended by** Mr. Eyre "will be **due entirely to Dr. Underhill's letter, and to** the delusions which **have been instilled into** the minds of

the ignorant peasantry by designing persons in reference to it." * And a day or two later he comments
on the "spirit of disaffection which existed in the
minds of the peasantry from the same causes." It
was all owing to the teaching of the Baptist ministers,
who dwelt among "an ignorant, debased, and excite-
able coloured population," endorsing and reiterating
such assertions as were contained in Dr. Underhill's
letter, especially in districts where the rebellion of
1831-32 broke out.

In fact, aided by an unscrupulous press, Mr. Eyre
had succeeded in rousing into activity that class
hatred which existed at emancipation, and which
of late years had in some measure been allayed,
but never eradicated. An old resident in Jamaica
fully corroborates this statement. He writes: "For
much of this spirit Mr. Eyre is responsible. Before
he commenced his unfortunate career, class and
complexional animosities were dying out, or seemed
to be. From the commencement of his administration as Governor they multiplied and grew, till at
length they have culminated in the present state of
things." † Government by and for the white minority
of the inhabitants had reached a crisis, and by the
foolish, one-sided, and often spiteful conduct of
Mr. Eyre and his Administration, had produced a
spirit of animosity and hostility to his rule which he
was unable to stem. Hence the bitterness with which
the current of obloquy was directed against his

---

* Papers, &c., pp. 235, 239, 256.
† The *Freeman*, July 19th, 1866.

political opponents, and against the Baptist missionaries in particular. The voices of the missionaries
were indeed scarcely heard in the din which Mr. Eyre's
use of the "infamous letter" had created. In but one
public meeting, that at Montego Bay, had any Baptist
minister taken chief or prominent part. A few of
them individually attended in other places, but they
contributed very little to the turmoil which sprang
from the passions and prejudices of the whites, or to
the outburst of that rankling sense of injury existing
among the blacks. The Baptist missionaries rarely
appeared as correspondents in the newspapers. Except in one or two instances they did not reply to the
vile calumnies and falsehoods heaped upon them.
They magnanimously bore reproach, assured, as the
result proved, that their rectitude and moderation,
the purity of their motives, and their freedom from
all just blame would be made to appear.

In the reign of terror which followed the riot at
Morant Bay, the Baptist missionaries were everywhere
taunted as the chief promoters of the "rebellion," as it
was called. The inflammatory language addressed by
Mr. Eyre to the Legislature called forth an intense
hostility against them. One native minister of their
number, the Rev. Edwin Palmer, a black man, already
referred to,* for a so-called seditious speech, was cruelly
and unjustly seized in Kingston and borne to Morant
Bay for trial, where he was exposed to horrible tortures
and the chance of death by the hands of the execu-

---

* See *ante*, Chapter X., p. 115.

tioners of Mr. Eyre's wrath. Nor were efforts wanting to bring the white missionaries within the grip of the cruel Provost Marshal Ramsay.

Their correspondence with the Mission House was violated. The senior Baptist missionary, a man universally known for his lofty Christian character, and a lover of peace, had four letters detained for several days, and was informed by the Postmaster that the letters of many others had been detained by the Governor's orders. Selected letters, or portions, of them, were sent to the Colonial Office, and attention directed to passages that it was thought by Mr. Eyre might be used to criminate the writers. In his despatch of the 23rd October,* he tells Mr. Cardwell that the "rebellion" had been stirred up "by the indiscreet acts, language, or writings of persons of education, as well as by political demagogues and agitators. Chief amongst these, I regret to say, are the Secretary of the Baptist Missionary Society in England, Dr. Underhill, and some of the Baptist ministers in Jamaica, who have endorsed and enlarged upon his views and statements." "The Governor and the whole force of the Government officials are against us," says a missionary, writing to Dr. Underhill in November. "Our conduct is carefully watched ; the Press, with only one exception, is bitter in its opposition ; we are afraid to write to you with our accustomed freedom." † Another, writing

---

* Papers on the Disturbances, Part I., p. 46, No. 253, received by the Colonial Office, November 17th, 1865.

† *Missionary Herald*, 1866, p. 8.

me on the same date, says : " In advocating as you did the cause of the poor, you committed an offence for which you never will be forgiven. Deep, bitter hatred will ever be the reward meted out to those who dare to point out to the negro that he might be better employed than working upon a sugar estate for sixpence or ninepence a day." Bearing in mind the imminent jeopardy, it was imagined, in which the Colony " was placed " by their proceedings, for Mr. Cardwell's information, Mr. **Eyre** enclosed one of my letters which he had intercepted. It was written to one of the marked men, the Rev. J. E. Henderson. From this letter Mr. Eyre quotes the following words as specially deserving condemnation : " In Jamaica, the people seem to be overwhelmed with discouragement, and I fear that they are giving up in despair their long struggle with injustice and fraud."

The Governor's comment on this sentence is too curious and suggestive to be passed by * :—

" If such language as this is addressed by the representative of the Baptist Missionary Society at home to its ministers out here, these ministers will naturally endeavour to give effect to the suggestion by stimulating the people not to ' give up the struggle,' whilst they will, no doubt, reckon and enlarge upon the alleged ' injustice and fraud,' as some of them have already done at the meeting at Montego Bay and elsewhere."

---

* **Blue Book. Further** Correspondence, 10th August, 1866, p. 50. **Address to Lord Russell.**

"The result is obvious, and, as instanced in the massacre at Morant Bay, in the outbreak of rebellion through an extensive tract of country, and in the disaffection and disloyalty which exist in so many parishes, and make it a question whether the rebellion may not become general throughout the entire island."

"If nothing can be done to stop at home the pernicious writings such as I refer to, and if Jamaica is to be retained at all, it will be necessary to pass a law in the Colony authorising the deportation of all persons who, leaving their proper sphere of action as ministers of religion, become political demagogues and dangerous agitators."

The monstrous proposition here made found no sympathy in the Colonial Office. I remained unmolested. A communication from Mr. Cardwell informing me of the stoppage and violation of my correspondence led to an interview on the subject with the Secretary of State, by my colleague, the Rev. F. Trestrail. The following are extracts from the despatch to Mr. Eyre, which Mr. Cardwell immediately wrote * :—

"At a moment when the Colony was placed, as you say, in imminent jeopardy, it was doubtless within the discretion of the executive authorities to resort to such a measure."

"I trust, however, that order having been restored, no further interception of letters, passing either to or

---

* Papers on Disturbances, Part I., p. 244, No. 353.

from the Colony, will have been thought necessary. It is only under very exceptional circumstances that such a departure from ordinary practice can be justified."

" The letter from Dr. Underhill has been returned to the writer, and I have to instruct you to forward any other letters which may have been detained to the person for whom they were destined, unless in any instance you should have the strongest reasons for believing that serious mischief would follow."

" The measure you suggest is not one to which I should wish you to have recourse. The repression of overt proceedings might lead to secret proceedings, not less, but more dangerous."

Previous to the receipt of this despatch, Mr. Eyre had actually given orders for the arrest of my correspondent, the Rev. J. E. Henderson. This deed of wrong was only stayed by the officer charged with its execution requiring from His Excellency a written order instead of the verbal one he had received. This Mr. Eyre refused, fearing, doubtless, to commit himself to a written paper which might become proof against him in a criminal prosecution. He did not, however, wait for Mr. Cardwell's reply to obtain, by a law from his moribund Legislature, the arbitrary power, as it might please him, of deporting any obnoxious individual. Only Mr. Eyre's suspension from his office as Governor prevented its wide application. My excellent and worthy friend, the Rev. J. M. Phillippo, of Spanish Town, was one among several others, both lay and clerical, whose names were already inscribed on a black list for proscription and exile. And another, whose honoured name was never mentioned but with respect and confidence, received a friendly intimation that he had need be careful, for he was suspected of sympathy with the rebels.* But it is worthy of note that in the political trials which afterwards took place, only one Baptist minister, a black man, Mr. Palmer, was arrested, and tried, and convicted of sedition by a common jury packed for the purpose. Not a single member of the Baptist churches was indicted by the officers of the Crown.† Had I been a resident in Jamaica, there can be little doubt what my lot would have been. Happily, I was beyond the reach of the interested attentions of Governor Eyre, and the tender mercies of his satellite, Provost Marshal Ramsay.

At the best, however, the vindication of the missionaries by the Commissioners, such as it was,‡ cannot be said to be sufficient. It did not meet the facts of the case. The allegations of Mr. Eyre, in his numerous despatches to the Colonial Office, were in the main unknown till they met the public eye in the Blue Books published for the information of the British

---

* *Missionary Herald*, 1866, p. 11.

† Memorial of Baptist Union. Blue Book, June 29th, 1866, p. 14.

‡ To a motion made by Mr. George Phillippo for the examination of the Revs. B. Millard and D. J. East, to reply to the statements of Mr. Eyre, the Commissioners replied "that there were no charges against Dr. Underhill or his Mission to require the Commissioners' interference at this stage." (Blue Book, Papers, &c., p. 19.)

Parliament, to say nothing of the calumnies adopted and circulated by the English Press. Under these circumstances, and as soon as the course resolved upon by the Royal Commissioners was understood, a very large proportion of the Baptist ministers and their congregations, some thirty in number, during the months from February to June, addressed memorials, some to the Queen, some to Lord Russell (then at the head of the Government), and others to the chief of the Colonial Office, by the hands of Sir Henry Storks, denying in forcible but dignified language the unjust allegations of Ex-Governor Eyre, and complaining of the gross aspersions on their Christian character which had fallen so freely from Mr. Eyre's inconsiderate pen.

It would be difficult to summarise or to state in detail the contents of these numerous memorials. It must suffice to say that they denied in firm and earnest language the Governor's assertions as to their conduct. They affirmed that on inquiry it would be found that no Baptist missionary congregation, white or black, existed in the Parish of St. Thomas-in-the-East. That not a single member of their churches, there or elsewhere, was either arrested or charged with having taken part or had the slightest complicity in the disturbances at Morant Bay. That only one black minister connected with the Mission, the Rev. Edwin Palmer, of Kingston, was tried for seditious language used at an " Underhill Meeting," uttered five months before the outbreak. One other coloured Baptist missionary, the Rev. James Service, living in

another parish, was arrested without the shadow of a
ground of suspicion. After a few days he was acquitted
with honour, not having even been brought to trial.
They pointed out that the " rebellion," so called, was
strictly local, both in its commencement and progress,
and that the population among whom they laboured
was ever loyal, and untouched by a seditious or evil
spirit. As teachers of religion, they say, they have
taught their hearers " the value of human life by the
price paid for its redemption by the Lord Jesus, and
not only to be loyal, but grateful to your Majesty's
Government." They are neither factious nor discontented with the Queen's rule, however much they
feel and complain of the misrule and injustice of the
Jamaica authorities; and they add, " We would most
solemnly renew to your Most Gracious Majesty our
assurance that we are and ever have been your
Majesty's peaceful and loyal subjects, valuing the
blessings of civil and religious liberty too highly to
hazard them, by insubordination to the laws under
which we live, and to the authorities your Majesty has
placed over us." They recall with grateful satisfaction
the testimony of several of Mr. Eyre's predecessors to
the loyalty they have ever shown, to their quiet
demeanour under circumstances of great trial, and to
their industry and improvement both in a physical
and social aspect since their release from the bondage
of slavery. They point to the settlements they have
made, to the villages they have built, to the homesteads they have acquired, to the culture of products
other than sugar for their own sustenance and for

12

export, and, finally, to the flourishing schools and institutions they enjoy, as the fruit of their own exertions, with the beneficent aid of their ministers.*

But urgent as were these representations of the many thousands of loyal men, and of ministers of the Gospel, eminent for their fidelity to their calling, the following was the only recognition they received of the justice of their appeal. It came from Lord Carnarvon, the Colonial Secretary of the new Administration, which, in the latter part of the year, held the reins of government in Great Britain. " Parliament," he writes, to Sir John Peter Grant, the new Governor, "has been put in possession of despatches by your predecessor (Sir Henry Storks), expressing a high sense of the services rendered to Jamaica by the great majority of the Baptist missionaries employed there, as well as a condemnation of the conduct of some of those missionaries. With those despatches the counter-statements of the Baptist missionaries have also been presented to Parliament, and thus all persons who take interest in the question will have the materials for arriving at a conclusion."

---

* On a review of the entire course taken by the missionaries, the Committee of the Baptist Missionary Society thus expressed themselves :—" They only repeat the judgment of all impartial men when they affirm that there was not the shadow of an excuse for the obnoxious and calumnious charges made against them by the late Governor, and that the ordeal through which they have passed has left their honour unstained, their integrity untouched, and their Christian character undimmed." (Report for 1867, p. 90.)

"I can only say that I gladly accept the assurances by the memorialists of their loyalty, and trust that for the future Her Majesty's Government may rely on their co-operation, both as regards the religious, moral, and social training of their flocks, and by the example which they have it in their power to give to the people of respect for the institutions of the country, and willing obedience to all constituted authority." *

Before leaving this part of my subject, I may be permitted to quote the language of Mr. Cardwell, spoken by him in the House of Commons, in the course of the debate on Jamaica affairs.† He says :—

"Before I sit down I wish to allude to another subject which should not pass unnoticed. It will be remembered that in the first despatch, in which Governor Eyre spoke of the principal causes of the disturbances, he alluded to a letter which had been addressed to me by Dr. Underhill, and he attributed to that letter, in great part, the origin of the disturbances. That letter having obtained publicity in Jamaica entirely through me, I feel bound to express my opinion on that part of the case. From the letter itself I very much dissent. It has been the subject of inquiry, the result of which is on the table. The letter was brought to me by my honourable friend the member for Bristol (Sir Morton Peto), was a *bonâ fide* letter, and addressed to me for the

* Further Correspondence presented to Parliament, August 10th, 1866, p. 58.
† Speech in the House of Commons, September 30th. 1866.

12*

purpose of obtaining practical inquiry into the **subject.** I accordingly sent **it to** the Governor for that purpose. **If** the consequences which have been said since **to** have resulted from that letter could **have** been reasonably expected by the Governor of Jamaica, I do not think **it was necessary to** give the letter publicity. I must say, too, with respect **to** the persons connected with that letter, that their conduct has been most moderate and reasonable; and of all the deputations which came to me there was none more temperate and calm in dealing with the subject than **a** deputation of Baptists, which came from different **parts of** the country, in company with the honourable member from Bristol." *

The result of this examination of the Report of the **Royal** Commissioners makes it abundantly clear that **the** Baptist missionaries had not, directly or indirectly, **any part** whatever in producing or aiding the outbreak at Morant **Bay.** In fact, the Baptist Missionary Society had no connection whatever with the Parish of St. Thomas-in-the-East. This arose, however, from no lack of effort in earlier times to secure a footing there. It may be seen from Dr. Coke's History of the West Indies, and the works of Duncan and Samuel, that a fierceness of opposition to the Gospel raged **in this parish** more strongly **than** in **any** other part of **the island.** It was the fixed determination of magistrates and rectors, both before and after emancipation, **to allow no Baptists, if they could prevent it, to enter**

---

* See *Missionary Herald*, 1866, p. 164.

that parish. The devoted missionary, Joseph Burton, once attempting it, was thrown into gaol, and was only released on very heavy bail being taken that he would come no more. A few faithful men of other denominations who visited the district were also bitterly persecuted, and the results of their ministry were but small. Four-fifths of the people were without religious instruction at all, and much of the hatred incurred by Mr. Gordon arose from his endeavours to secure for the population the preaching of the Gospel, and from his efforts to disseminate Divine truth.*

During the course of the proceedings of the Royal Commissioners, several of the Baptist missionaries in attendance had opportunities of intercourse with the Commissioners. On one of these occasions the Rev. D. J. East informed Sir Henry Storks that throughout the whole of the disturbed district there was no agent of the Baptist Missionary Society; that the only recognised Baptist minister in its neighbourhood was a native, who, so far from having any complicity with the riot, had to seek refuge on board one of H.M. ships; but not one European. Sir Henry expressed his regret that this was so, and his hope that in the future the Society would again endeavour to enter on this field of labour; and added, " If I had the keys of the Treasury you should not want for funds."

This favourable opinion encouraged the Jamaica Baptist Missionary Society to appoint the Rev. J. M.

---

* See *Missionary Herald*, January, 1866, p. 7.

Phillippo and the Rev. T. Lea to visit the district, and
on the 1st March they entered on their task. They
reported of one fertile and beautiful spot, that they
found the inhabitants ignorant, superstitious, and, with
few exceptions, " far from God, by wicked works."
They were suspicious and discouraged, yet received
the messengers with hopeful confidence. As they
passed along they met with most piteous tales of
mourning, lamentation, and woe, and saw on every
side the sad evidences of destruction, the work of an
infuriated and irresponsible soldiery. In the district
around Morant Bay there lived a dense population,
morally dark and degraded. So far as any religious
feeling was expressed, the people said they were Baptists, and were not disposed to unite with any other
community. But they would welcome the representatives of the Baptist Mission, and rejoice to have public
worship and schools set up in their midst by them.

The conviction was impressed on the minds of the
deputation that the opportunity was most favourable
to renew the attempt made in times gone by, and to
send an earnest and experienced missionary to Morant
Bay, " who, by his life and teaching, may diffuse the
holy influences of the religion of Jesus in the places
where so recently anarchy and bloodshed held their
sway, and have left behind the most lamentable
results." *

Supported by letters from several missionaries,
these facts were laid before the Home Committee,

---

* *Missionary Herald*, July, 1866, pp. 119-122.

who, also encouraged in a subsequent interview, enjoyed by their Treasurer and Secretary, with Sir Henry Storks, at once resolved on the appointment of the Rev. W. Teall, of Lucea, who, by his energy and devotedness, was well qualified for the task. They voted for the primary expenses the sum of £250, undertaking also to support the work for seven years, or until the result of the labours of the missionary should be successful in the formation of a self-supporting church.

The introduction of the Mission was hailed by all parties in the parish. The times were changed. The black people were jubilant. The new Custos engaged to do all in his power to protect and aid Mr. Teall. His coming was regarded with pleasure, even by those whose enmity in earlier days had been so unhappily displayed. His first visit to Stony Gut was a most affecting one. He preached to a large congregation on the spot where Paul Bogle's chapel had stood. The widows of the two Bogles, George Clarke (the brother of the Samuel Clarke who was hung at Morant Bay), and a host of women and children, clothed in mourning, crowded around him. At the close of the service, George Clarke thus addressed the congregation:—"My friends," he said, "all the wrongs which so many of us have suffered unjustly at the hands of the authorities and soldiers, I know I speak your sentiments as well as my own when I say, we freely forgive, as well as all who have injured us in any way." To which there was the hearty response of "Amen."

In July, 1868, the Society purchased a **disused** chapel **in** Morant Bay, and the work thus established **has now** become **the** scene **of** a flourishing church and schools, **and has** extended its beneficent action in all directions **around this central spot.** The unhappy **events we have narrated are** not, indeed, forgotten ; **but** God has been pleased to lead many **of the** people into the paths of righteousness **and** peace. Their mourning has been turned into joy.

CHAPTER XIV.

BEFORE closing this account of the work of the Royal Commissioners, it is of some importance to record its reception by the English Government, and the results which followed in this country.

The two Commissioners, Messrs. Gurney and Maule, arrived in England on the 28th April, bringing with them their united Report. Sir H. Storks remained in Jamaica to induct his successor into the office which Sir Henry had so ably and temporarily filled. At the close of their inquiries, the Commissioners left the island in a state of perfect quietude, the more remarkable when contrasted with the excitement and terror in which they found it four months before On the north side the sugar estates were in full crop, and the crops were larger than they had been for many years. The demand for labour was urgent everywhere, and all capable hands found full employment. Order prevailed in every district. The expected change of Government was joyfully looked forward to by all parties. The administration of justice had been carefully watched by Sir Henry

Storks, who by circular had required all magistrates, either to give regular and prompt attention to their duties, or to resign their commissions. A goodly number of resignations of the most unworthy of them speedily followed.

But attention must now be given to the views of Her Majesty's Government at home. These are found in a despatch from the Hon. E. Cardwell, addressed to Sir Henry Storks, on the 18th June, the very day on which Lord Russell's Reform measure was rejected by the House of Commons, and a week before the resignation of office by his entire Ministry. Generally, the Government, writes Mr. Cardwell, concurs in the conclusions arrived at by the Commissioners, and approves of the commendation bestowed upon the skill, promptitude, and vigour displayed by Mr. Eyre in the early stages of the insurrection, to which must be attributed, in a great degree, its speedy termination. The causes which led to the resistance to lawful authority must be reserved for future consideration, in conjunction with the new Government about to be established in Jamaica.

In judging of the excessive nature of the punishments inflicted, Mr. Cardwell considers that the "greatest consideration" is due to a Governor placed in the peculiar position of Mr. Eyre. The insurrection was sudden; its extent was unknown. It took the character of a contest of colour. The nature of the atrocities committed, and the enormous disparity of numbers between the white and black population, had to be taken into account. It was difficult to discriminate the false from the true in the number-less rumours that ran from place to place, while the forces at hand for the suppression of the outbreak were but small, and inadequate to control every district. Mr. Eyre properly felt that the most serious consequences might ensue from the slightest in-decision. He also wisely resisted the advice of his Council to place the whole island under martial law, and showed himself superior to the feelings of alarm entertained by those around him.

On the other hand, it is pointed out that martial law, though limited in its range, and confined to the statutable time, was continued for many days after it could have been dispensed with. For after the first two or three days no serious outrages were committed by the insurgents, nor was any resistance at all offered to the troops. On the 20th October, the day Governor Eyre departed from Morant Bay, leaving Gordon to the mercy of the Court-Martial, he wrote to Mr. Cardwell that he was satisfied the rebellion was got under ; and on the 30th, a fortnight before the expira-tion of martial law, it was formally stated in the proclamation of amnesty that the " wicked rebellion" existing in certain parts of the County of Surrey had been subdued. The insurgents, it was said, were desirous to return to their allegiance, and the chief instigators of the rebellion had suffered the punish-ments their heinous offences deserved. For these reasons Her Majesty's Government cannot but concur in the judgment of the Commissioners, that martial law and its severities had been continued longer than necessity required.

Three if not four weeks before its close, prisoners could have been arraigned, and sufficiently punished, by the ordinary tribunals, and a calm inquiry might and ought to have been substituted for the violence and arbitrariness of the military power. Numbers were executed who were neither ringleaders of the insurrection, nor participators in the crimes committed at the commencement of the outbreak. Nor did the circumstances justify the wholesale floggings and burning of the houses of the people. Public safety did not require these pitiless deeds. Her Majesty's Government were therefore unable to regard Mr. Eyre as "irresponsible" for the unnecessary suspension of the ordinary judicial procedure. Blame must rest upon him for permitting the severities which attended the reprehensible measures adopted on his authority. Especially does this apply to the case of Mr. Gordon, whose unjust condemnation Her Majesty's Government "cannot but deplore and condemn." As suggested by Mr. Westmorland, Mr. Gordon might well have been reserved for trial by a regular tribunal, and "have enjoyed the means of defence which are secured by the ordinary process of law to every subject of the Queen." Having regard to all the circumstances of the case, and also to other portions of Mr. Eyre's conduct while administering the affairs of the island, of which they had been compelled to disapprove, the Government felt it to be their duty to advise the

Crown not to replace Mr. Eyre in the Government of Jamaica.*

In simply dismissing Mr. Eyre **from his** office **as** Governor of Jamaica, and also from future employment **in the** civil service of the Crown, the Ministry of Lord **Russell** was to my knowledge actuated by the fact, **that the** Government felt themselves under **a certain amount of** obligation to him for seizing **the** opportunity to effect an entire change **in the system** of government **in** operation in Jamaica. **In this** despatch, **Mr.** Cardwell speaks with approval of **the** promptitude and **judgment** Mr. Eyre had shown in obtaining **from** the Jamaica Legislature **the** abolition **of** all their privileges as a self-governing Colony, by **which the English Government were** enabled **to inaugurate** a new **administration under the direct control** of the Crown. The change **had** long **been** desired. **Several** attempts, since the period of emancipation, **had been** made **to bring the** administration **of** the **Colony into harmony with the** new conditions created by **that great act of justice and** mercy. Mr. Eyre had accomplished **what** all former **Governors had failed to do; and, though it was achieved during a state of craven panic, it was not the less a** welcome **relief from the perplexities and strained** relations **which had so long** existed **between the Home** and Colonial **Governments.** The **island had** fallen into an un**exampled condition of poverty and distress,** and grave forebodings **were prevalent of its speedy ruin.** Some

---

* **Blue Book:** Further Correspondence, 10th August, **1866,** p. 92.

consideration was doubtless due to Mr. Eyre for his success in this respect, and it fully accounts for the reluctance displayed by the Government of Lord Russell to sanction any judicial inquiry into the faults and crimes of his administration.

In one point only did the Government lean towards any semblance of severity. Sir Henry Storks was instructed not to give a certificate of indemnity to any one who had exceeded his instructions, and they further directed the trial of persons charged with real enormities—as, for instance, the Provost Marshal Ramsay. It is not possible to say what the Government of Lord Russell would have done to meet the loud demand, which immediately rose on the publication of the Report from a very large proportion of their party, to bring Mr. Eyre to trial before an English Court, charged with the death of Mr. Gordon and of others who had been convicted on insufficient and illegal evidence.

But the Conservative party were now in power, under the leadership of the Earl of Derby, with Lord Carnarvon as his Colonial Secretary. The opportunity of learning the decision of the new Government soon arose in the House of Commons, in the discussion which was called forth by a series of resolutions proposed by Mr. E. Buxton, on the 31st July. His first resolution affirmed "that this House deplores the excessive punishments which followed the suppression of the disturbances of October last, in the Parish of St. Thomas, Jamaica, and especially the unnecessary frequency with which the punishment of death was inflicted." The second resolution approved the dismissal of Mr. Eyre from his governorship, and the concurrence of the House in the view of the late Colonial Secretary, that while minor offences might be overlooked, still greater offenders ought to be punished, and excesses of severity in the suppression should not be passed over with impunity. And, lastly, that compensation should be awarded to those whose property had been wantonly and cruelly destroyed.

It need scarcely to be said that the speeches of Mr. Buxton, Mr. Mills, and others were worthy of the occasion. The mouthpiece of the Government was Mr. Adderley, Under Secretary of State. He professed fully to recognise the gravity of the events in Jamaica, and proceeded to treat the Commission as a fully constituted tribunal for the trial of the facts, of which the Report was "the only authentic information they possessed." The Government, however, were not "going to re-open the case and try it again." The House was not a judicial tribunal (nor for the matter of that was the Commission). The Report must be taken as it is given, and Mr. Buxton's "resolutions ought not to be adopted." In concluding his speech Mr. Adderley moved the previous question, as if the acts done in Jamaica were worthy of praise, and in order to avoid even the appearance of deploring the official slaughter. This was too gross a condonation of the crimes admitted to have been committed. Mr. Adderley's resolution was negatived, but he finally assented to the adoption of the first resolution.

Thus, so far as the Government of Great Britain

could accomplish it, the final appeal to the Imperial
Parliament, to judge between the negro subjects of
the Queen and the officials who so mercilessly
scourged them and put them to death, was set at
nought. The House would weep over these atrocities,
but it declined to punish the authors of them. It
is unnecessary to go over the sickening story again;
but it was resolved that, so far as the Government and
Parliament could determine, the guilt of the perpe-
trators should go unpunished, and the terrible injustice
pass away unavenged. For the astounding catalogue
of crimes recorded by the Commissioners, there
should be no judicial or even political remedy, though
not one tittle of the facts was denied or disproof
attempted. With regard to Mr. Gordon, Mr. Commissioner Gurney said that even if the evidence
against him might have justified an indictment for
sedition, "it did not justify the sentence passed upon
him and unfortunately carried into execution." It
was painful to think that he was carried from a
Queen's ship, whence all Jamaica could not have
rescued him, to be put to death,* without a voice
being heard in his defence.

---

* See the *Spectator* of August 4th, 1866.

CHAPTER XV.

PART I.

THE TRIAL OF PROVOST MARSHAL RAMSAY.

OF all the instruments employed by Mr. Eyre in the "retribution" and punishment inflicted on the alleged rebels, no one attained a more dreadful notoriety than Provost Marshal Ramsay. The story of his cruelties, of the scourgings and hangings of the unfortunate peasantry who fell into his hands, as recorded in the evidence, would fill many pages. But apart from his share in the execution of Mr. Gordon, and many other innocent sufferers, there is one example which stands out beyond all others for its savagery and brutal callousness, and its utter illegality. By the direction of the Colonial Office he was arraigned for this crime, before the Special Commission of Oyer and Terminer, assembled at Kingston, for wilful murder. The case to be tried was that of George Marshall, residing in Morant Bay, a coloured man, but not a negro. The reporter of the *Colonial Standard*, Mr. Lake, states that his offence was that he was met, on October 18th, without a pass in his possession from the Provost Marshal. In the inquiry before the Royal Commission the accusation brought

13

forward was that he was seen by a policeman carrying
some woollen goods, presumably stolen, but of which
there was not a particle of evidence. The charge was
an afterthought; it was not adduced at the time.
Without trial or investigation, as no pass could be
found upon him, he was treated as a rebel. He was
tied to a gun and flogged by three sailors from H.M.S.
Wolverine. " On receiving the forty-seventh or forty-
eighth lash he turned round and ground his teeth.
The Provost Marshal saw him, and ordered him to be
hanged immediately. His hands were so tied that
he could make no gesture. His back was like a bit
of raw beef, bleeding very profusely. He was taken
down, thrown on his back, his hands and feet tied, a
rope put round his neck and thrown over a rail, and
then he was hoisted up as you would a barrel of flour.
He had no drop. After about three minutes a huge
white stone was taken and put between his arms,
which were tied behind him." *

So far the evidence of the journalist.

Mr. Daniel Marshallack, a magistrate and store
keeper at Morant Bay, corroborates this ghastly story.

" I was sitting at my house, and I heard that a man
was to be flogged. I went out in the Parade, in company with another party, and I saw a man by the
name of Marshall being tied. He was tied to a gun
and flogged. He had a great number of lashes given
to him; I think very nearly fifty. I did not count
them, but there was a great number of lashes. The

---

* Report of Royal Commission, p. 275. Further Correspondence, &c., p. 16.

man shrieked a little, and drew up his body; and I immediately heard the Provost Marshal, Mr. Ramsay, say, 'Take down that man and hang him.' The man was immediately taken down. He was so weak that he could scarcely walk. He was pulled along, and when he got just under the hanging place he was pulled up. A rope was put round his neck as he was lying down, or very nearly so. He could scarcely stand. And he was pulled up and hanged, just as a barrel would be hoisted up by the side of a ship." Very significantly the witness adds, in reply to a question whether he informed anybody, "No one dared to say a word. The magistrates and every person of respectability were treated with the utmost disrespect. They were not solicited nor asked a single question." *

For this cruel and savage crime the Government of Jamaica ordered the prosecution of the Provost Marshal in the Commission Court. The Grand Jury, happily for him, was composed chiefly of planters and book-keepers from the sugar estates. On the 18th October, 1866, the very day twelvemonth on which the crime was committed, the case was called on. With the above evidence in his hands, the Hon. Judge Kerr charged the Grand Jury. He stated that under the ordinary law, the treatment of Marshall consti-tuted "a murder of the purest type." "Martial law,"

---

* Report of Royal Commission, p. 57. On the same day, Ramsay attempted to hang two other men, without trial; but his intention was frustrated by the intervention of one of the officers of the *Wolverine.*

13*

he said, " is the recurrence to physical force for the bringing about of results beyond the scope and capabilities of the ordinary law." Acts in themselves unlawful under the ordinary law must, therefore, be justified by the special exigency of the case. But even martial law does not authorise or sanction every deed assumed to be done in its name. It stops far short of that. Men, otherwise innocent of crime, may suffer from mere gratified malice, hatred and ill-will, lust and rapacity."

The limits of martial law can be thus defined. First, it allows all that is necessary to the suppression of resistance to lawful authority. Second, it requires that the acts done under it should be honest and *bona fide,* or they will be disallowed. Thirdly, the acts of its agents " shall be adjudged to be necessary in the judgment, not of a violent or excited, but of a moderate and reasonable man. Reason and common sense must approve the particular act. It is not sufficient that the party so acting should unaffectedly believe such and such a line of conduct to be called for: the belief must be reasonably entertained, and such as a person of ordinary understanding would not repudiate." Vindictive passions must have no place. They are as much prohibited during military rule as in the most orderly, tranquil condition of human affairs. " Excess and wantonness, cruelty and unscrupulous contempt for human life meet with no sanction from martial law any more than from ordinary law. No amount of personal provocation will justify or excuse vindictive retribution."

The learned Judge concluded by warning the Grand Jury that the Indemnity Act, with which the Jamaica Legislature had lately wound up its baneful legislation, "could only be pleaded in a court of justice by those who have fulfilled the conditions above stated."

True to their evil history, the Jamaica Grand Jury, in the teeth of the clear statements and recommendation of the Judge, refused to bring in a true bill, or to submit the clearly unlawful and criminal acts of Provost Marshal Ramsay to a petty jury.* The lucid, temperate, constitutional, and impartial charge of the Judge availed nothing, and this case of awful crime has passed into history unpunished and unavenged. After fifteen minutes' consultation, the prisoner was discharged from custody, and walked out of Court with the Victoria Cross upon his breast, won in the mad cavalry charge up the heights of Balaclava, a disgrace to the profession to which he belonged.†

Ramsay was, however, dismissed by Sir J. P. Grant from employment as Inspector of Police, and from all public employment soon after his arrival, the Governor recording in his minute:—"I cannot guess the ground on which the Grand Jury thought it their duty to contradict the Judge's charge by their finding. It carried to every unprejudiced mind the conviction of his guilt."‡ There can be no doubt, said Lord

---

° Further Correspondence, &c., May 28th, 1867, p. 11.

† The *Freeman* of November 16th, 1866, pp. 472, 575.

‡ Despatch of November 8th, 1866 ; Blue Book, May, 1867, p. 23 ; also Despatch of November 16th, No. 89, p. 46.

Carnarvon, that the course of justice has been griev-
ously defeated in this case.

It was the Colonial Minister's opinion that it was
of no use to carry these proceedings further, and all
efforts to bring to trial, parties guilty of similar acts of
cruelty, were abandoned.

PART II.

PROCEEDINGS OF THE JAMAICA COMMITTEE.

This miscarriage of justice in Jamaica, in the case
of Ramsay, rendered it the more necessary that an
attempt should be made, in this country, to bring
some of the parties engaged in the suppression of the
disturbances before an ordinary civil tribunal, both to
test the validity of the courts-martial under which
these crimes were committed, and to visit with due
punishment the parties guilty of them. For this
purpose the case of Mr. George William Gordon was
selected by the Jamaica Committee. It was thought
to be the most flagrant example of an innocent person
done to death by these courts, and which, if permitted to pass unnoticed, would render insecure the
life of every British subject throughout the world.

The treatment that Mr. Stuart Mills' appeal to
Parliament, and the resolutions of Mr. Buxton,
received at the hands of Lord Derby's Government
rendered it certain that it would neither prosecute
any of the parties inculpated, nor give any sanction
to proceedings against them by others. So far as the

authorities of the Crown were concerned, the Government was resolved to take no notice of the findings of the Royal Commission, and to oppose all judicial inquiry into the conduct of the military forces of the Crown, however serious were the infractions proved or declared to have been committed on the constitutional privileges of the Queen's subjects.

The Jamaica Committee were not, and could not, be actuated by vindictive feelings. They were a body of honourable men, held in high public estimation, and representative of the best elements of England's political life. It was their anxious desire, in the first place, " to establish, by a judicial sentence, the principle that the illegal execution of a British subject, by a person in authority, is not merely an error which superiors in office may at their discretion visit with displeasure or condone, but a crime which will certainly be punished by the law." In the second place, it was their object to challenge in a court of justice " the jurisdiction of courts of martial law, which, as late events showed, may be made engines of indiscriminate butchery and torture, and to examine their claim to try charges of high treason or other civil offences in the absence of a jury or any adequate security for justice, and without necessarily keeping a record of their proceedings ; whether, in fact, the law which these courts assume to administer is really law at all, or a truly sanguinary licence, which the law will repress or punish." *

* Jamaica Papers, No. 3, Statement of Committee, p. 4.

The refusal of Lord Russell's Government to reinstate Mr. Eyre in his office of Governor gave to the Committee, in common with multitudes of their fellow-citizens, little satisfaction on the first point and none at all as regards the second. It was not that Lord Derby's Government approved of Mr. Gordon's execution, or of the unnecessary severities inflicted by the soldiery and other officers of the courts; but they did not care to treat the proceedings at Morant Bay as infractions of constitutional law. They would leave the definition of the law of England with regard to martial law to stand as bluntly stated by Mr. Disraeli in his reply to Mr. Mill, that martial law is the suspension of all law, and exposes the lives of British subjects to irresponsible butchery.

It is advisable, in order to understand what follows, briefly to recapitulate the main facts of the case of Mr. Gordon, on which the Committee relied, to justify the prosecution of Ex-Governor Eyre and his subordinates. The following facts were admitted on all hands to be indubitable. Mr. Gordon had for years been in a position of strained political antagonism to the Administration of which Mr. Eyre was the head. There was no military necessity for taking his life. He was living out of the reach of military law, and within the jurisdiction of the civil courts. He had taken no part in the outbreak. Mr. Eyre personally arrested him, which he had no ministerial right to do. He accompanied him to the spot where military law prevailed, kept him in his own custody for several days, till he could deliver him over to the military tribunal. The Governor would not listen to the voice of warning raised by a member of his Council, who admitted the reason of his advice to be that, on the nature of the evidence that could be produced, a fatal verdict would not be assured in Kingston, where Gordon was known and respected, and where legal assistance was at hand. The composition of the Court-Martial was such as to cut off all hope alike of justice or mercy. * Mr. Gordon was further deprived of legal advice, which, when furnished in a letter by Mr. Wemys Anderson, his private solicitor, was refused, and the letter never delivered to Gordon. No delay was permitted in order to obtain the local evidence within reach, or otherwise easily procurable for his defence. The evidence adduced against him was palpably "insufficient," and some of it contradictory. The Royal Commissioners were convinced that the charge of conspiracy could not be sustained, since there was no proof that a conspiracy ever existed. They also affirm that much of the evidence given against Mr. Gordon was "inadmissible according to the rules that regulate evidence in English courts, either civil or military."† In fact, they declare that the evidence, oral and documentary, was wholly insufficient to establish the charge upon which the prisoner was put upon his trial. Nevertheless, the sentence was death. It was warmly approved by Governor Eyre, who took the responsibility of it, although he knew that the insurrection was at an

---

* Jamaica Papers, No. 3, Statement of Committee, p. 4.
† Report of Royal Commission, p. 36.

end, and the plea of military necessity was no longer of any force.

Such, in brief outline, was the case as it presented itself to the Jamaica Committee, and in the impartial judgment of the Royal Commissioners. Not only was this view sustained by many men of great legal knowledge, but the Committee were also confirmed in the propriety of the course they determined upon by the special opinion of the two eminent counsel by whom they were advised. These gentlemen held that " Mr. Gordon, with others, had been illegally put to death, or flogged, and in some cases flogged and afterwards put to death, and the homes of many others illegally burnt by Ex-Governor Eyre, Brigadier Nelson, and their subordinates and coadjutors." *

The first step taken was to apply at Bow Street Police Court for warrants to apprehend Brigadier Nelson and Lieutenant Brand, who were at the time within the jurisdiction of the Court. Ex-Governor Eyre would have been included in the summons but that he resided in Shropshire, and refused to place himself within reach of the prosecution. The application was made to Sir Thomas Henry, the Chief Magistrate at Bow Street, on the 6th February, 1867, by Mr. Fitzjames Stephen and Mr. Horne Payne, acting on behalf of the Jamaica Committee. Brigadier Nelson, it will be remembered, was the General Officer in command at Morant Bay at the time of Gordon's execution ; and Lieutenant Brand

---

* Jamaica Papers, No. 3, p. 3.

was the President of the Military Court, assisted by two young officers, before whom Gordon was arraigned. The solemn and grave responsibility assumed by this scratch tribunal may be gathered from a brief notice of its achievements. In the few days of their existence as a Court, its members sentenced 189 persons to be hung, and the execution was carried out with the briefest possible delay. Only twenty-five of the number were accused of murder. The rest were charged with "rebellion." Of these rebels, so-called, three were women. Of the whole number, 160 at least were not shown to have been engaged in any armed resistance to the authorities.[*] On the 30th October, Mr. Eyre declared the "rebellion" subdued; yet in numerous cases this military tribunal, after that date, continued to inflict the penalty of death, with the express sanction and approval of Brigadier Nelson. Not one of these victims was convicted of complicity with murder; only of "rebellion," and that on the most flimsy testimony.

Such was the case as laid before the Magistrate on this 6th February. Four days were devoted to the hearing of evidence and to the speeches of counsel. On the 23rd the warrants were issued and the accused arrested. Bail was accepted on their behalf, and they were ordered to appear at the Old Bailey Sessions to be held on the 8th April. The accused were not left without defence, the War Office and the Admiralty

---

[*] Mr. Buxton's Speech in the House of Commons.

furnishing the necessary counsel. In giving his decision Sir Thomas Henry gave the following reasons for his action :—" The arguments," he said, "which have been addressed to me afford abundant proof that there are doubtful and difficult questions of law, and disputed questions of fact, which must arise in this case. I purposely abstain from expressing any opinion of my own upon the painful case before me. It is enough for me to say that it is a case that demands further inquiry. It is my duty, therefore, to put it in train for that inquiry."

But before the day appointed for the trial the case of Ex-Governor Eyre requires attention.

PART III.

THE SHROPSHIRE MAGISTRATES AND EX-GOVERNOR EYRE.

However unwilling to face his accusers, the Ex-Governor was not to be allowed to escape, and on Monday, the 26th March, Mr. Fitzjames Stephen appeared before an ordinary Sessions Court for the County of Shropshire, held at Market Drayton. It consisted of Sir B. Leighton, Chairman of Quarter Sessions, assisted by five other county magistrates. Residing in the county, Mr. Eyre was within their jurisdiction. In his luminous address, Mr. Fitzjames Stephen cited the Acts of Parliament under which he claimed the issue of a warrant for Mr. Eyre's arrest, stating briefly the facts, and calling as witnesses several persons who had arrived from Jamaica for the purpose, **Dr.** Fiddes, **Lake, and** others. After considerable discussion the warrant **was issued,** and the Ex-Governor was ordered to appear before the Court on the Wednesday following. As the counsel for **Mr.** Eyre promised he should appear on the day appointed, the warrant was not actually executed.

The proceedings of **the Court were resumed on** Wednesday, the 28th, with the same Chairman, and four county magistrates on the Bench. The prosecutor on this occasion was Mr. **P.** Taylor, M.P. for Leicester, and a prominent supporter and member of the Jamaica Committee, the existence **of which was** most persistently ignored by the advocates of Mr. Eyre. In a very clear and masterly address, **Mr. Fitzjames Stephen** first dwelt on the general causes **of the** outbreak at Morant Bay, and, secondly, on the proof that the legal position of the ex-Governor was either that he **was** guilty of murder, **or** his acts constituted **a** case **of** justifiable homicide. **He** showed that Mr. **Eyre was** responsible for **the** proclamation of martial **law, and** for all the deeds **done under its** authority. **Indeed,** it was to the credit **of the Ex-Governor** that he had voluntarily and **honourably assumed this responsible** position, **and had fairly** acknowledged his entire responsibility. **But this did** not justify the putting **to death a man** who was not living under martial **law,** and had done **nothing to bring him** within its scope. There was no question that Mr. Eyre, owing to political differences, **had long entertained the most hostile** feelings against Mr. Gordon. He had on several occasions expressed the worst possible opinion of him years before these transactions occurred. He may have thought his treatment of Mr. Gordon was just— even a political necessity; but it was nevertheless illegal, and ought not to have been done, even to intimidate others with whom Mr. Gordon was supposed to have made common cause. Martial law does not, and cannot, justify the putting a man to death, who had no connection—no open and undoubted connection—with a state of insurrection among Her Majesty's subjects. Legal proof must be found that he was actually a party to the insurrection. Otherwise the execution was a murder. Mr. Eyre was, in fact, fully aware that his conduct was of doubtful legality.

The Court had to consider two questions: First, whether it was legal to take a civilian from a district not under martial law to one in which such a law prevailed; and secondly, whether Mr. Eyre's conduct towards Mr. Gordon was that of a man who only desired to punish treason. Mr. Eyre had allowed himself to form such an opinion of Gordon's character, personal and political,* that he really seemed to think that in

---

* Mrs. Gordon has furnished us with the following protest against Mr. Eyre's abuse of her husband received from many most respected residents in Jamaica :—" We, the undersigned, having resided in the island many years, and having had very considerable opportunities of knowing and forming an estimate of the late Mr. Gordon's character in his various relations, do hereby protest against the allegations as made by Mr. Eyre, and declare them to be utterly without foundation."—James

putting him to death he required hardly any legal justification at all, or anything else except his own judgment of what a bad and immoral man Gordon was.*

No evidence was called to rebut the arguments of Mr. Stephen or the statements of his witnesses, nor did Mr. Giffard, the counsel for Mr. Eyre, make any attempt to reply on the legal aspects of the case. His address was an appeal to the prejudices of his auditory, and the grave questions involved were quietly passed by. Mr. Giffard knew that the magistrates deeply sympathised with the bulk of their party, and it was with no surprise after a consultation of ten or fifteen minutes at the close of the counsel's speech, that the Bench delivered their decision to dismiss the case. Mr. Fitzjames Stephen's speech had been an exhaustive one, both as to the facts and the law, and remarkable for its erudition and eloquence. But Mr. Giffard's address appealed chiefly to the emotions of his hearers, and revelled in laudation of the Ex-Governor, and in abuse of the prosecution. There was an endeavour to perplex by raising irrelevant issues, and frequent in-

---

Phillippo, senior Baptist missionary; William Andrews, attorney-at-law; Robert Osborn, James Bell, Alexander Fiddes, F.R.C.S.; Andrew Lyon, Common Councilman of Kingston; Thomas Geddes, Savanna-la-Mar; James Scott, M.R.C.S.; Abraham Pinto, M. Ramos, merchants; Rev. R. Gordon, priest of the Church of England."

* In this *précis* of the proceedings at Market Drayton, I have followed the excellent reports of the *Daily News*, published at the time.

terruptions were encouraged in the course of Mr. Stephen's argument. The decision was a foregone conclusion and no one wondered at the result. It stood in strange contrast to the grave and weighty words of Sir Thomas Henry. The Shropshire Magistrates adjudged that " the evidence which has been adduced before us does not raise in our minds a strong or probable presumption of the guilty motives imputed to Edward John Eyre in the alleged murder of George William Gordon, and we are confident that if the same evidence was brought before a jury, a verdict of acquittal would be recorded. It now only remains for us to direct the discharge of Edward John Eyre. Mr. Eyre, you are discharged."

So a question which the learned and practised Judge of Bow Street, a man eminent for legal knowledge and impartiality, deemed to be of so serious a character as to require the verdict of a higher tribunal, was peremptorily and lightly dismissed, in defiance both of facts and law, by a Bench of county squires, who are not usually regarded as gifted with farsightedness, freedom from prejudice, or a knowledge of constitutional law. The proof of malice on the part of Mr. Eyre was overwhelming, to which point the decision of the Bench was arbitrarily confined, while the utter illegality of Gordon's arrest and execution was entirely ignored. However, the decision fully answered the purpose of shielding Mr. Eyre from suffering any other penalty than his dismissal from office, and the deep regrets which must have accompanied him into his retirement from the public service.

These county justices **did** not profess to inquire
into the law, or the validity of the Jamaica law of
indemnity. They simply despised the great weight of
the evidence laid before them, **and** refused to allow
the case to proceed to the stage at which it would
receive the enlightened exposition of **Her Majesty's**
superior courts.

In the case of Nelson and Brand it **was the opinion**
of both Sir Thomas Henry and of the Lord **Chief**
Justice, that the charge against them should go
forward to the higher tribunal. **How** much more
should that of Governor Eyre, seeing, on his own
admission, he was entirely responsible for the terrible
events at Morant **Bay.**

PART IV.

THE CHARGE OF LORD CHIEF JUSTICE COCKBURN.

On the opening **of the Old** Bailey Sessions Court
on the 10th April, it was **soon** filled by a profoundly
interested audience. Under ordinary circumstances,
the judge would have been **the** Recorder of **London,**
Mr. Russell Gurney; **but his** connection with the
case as a Royal Commissioner led to the substitution
of the Lord Chief Justice, who, on the Court as-
sembling, proceeded at once to deliver a charge to
the Grand **Jury of seven hours'** duration, listened to
throughout with the most strained attention. It was
subsequently printed with the revisal of the Lord

14

Chief Justice himself, and constitutes a work of the greatest authority, with regard to the nature and legality of martial law, within the compass of the British Empire. It is not possible to give here more than the conclusions to which Lord Cockburn came, for his charge ranged over the whole extent of the subject, both in its history and its modern application.

That such an inquiry was absolutely necessary, Lord Cockburn shows by the quotation of certain doctrines, "of the wildest and most startling" character, which he said had of late been put forward to justify Mr. Eyre's proceedings. Thus, "Martial law is arbitrary and uncertain in its nature, so much so that the term law cannot be properly applied to it." Again, "When martial law is proclaimed, the law is the will of the ruler, or rather the will of the ruler is law. Martial law is, in short, the suspension of all law." And he found in print this amazing proposition: "When martial law is proclaimed, there is no rule or law by which the officers executing martial law are bound to carry on their proceedings. It overrides all other law. It is entirely arbitrary." If such, said the Lord Chief Justice, is the character of the system of law under which British subjects can be tried for their lives or liberties, it is high time it should be brought to the test of judicial determination, and that Parliament should interpose and put some check upon a jurisdiction so purely arbitrary and capricious. But there is no authority at all for such doctrines. They are as unfounded and as untenable as they are mischievous. Such doctrines are repugnant to the genius of our people, to the spirit of our laws and institutions.* And it must not be forgotten that, whatever the crime with which a man is charged, he is still a subject and entitled to those safeguards which are of the essence of justice.

After tracing the history of martial law in this country, the Chief Justice remarks: " So far as I have been able to discover, no such thing as martial law has ever been put in force in this country against civilians, for the purpose of putting down rebellion.† So far as I can find it has never been resorted to or exercised in England for such a purpose at all." He next quotes the eminent judge, Lord Hale, as defining martial law to mean, " a law applying only to members of the army, and not intended to be applied to others who were not bound by a military constitution, but were to be governed only by the ordinary law, though it were in time of war."‡ With which judgment other sages in English law agree.

Even under martial law there is nothing arbitrary or capricious. The accusation must be distinctly specified. The evidence must be such as an ordinary court would receive. The accused must enjoy the fullest opportunity of defence. The witnesses must be confronted with him, and cross-examination allowed. But if this be granted to a soldier, bound by his military oath, much more must it be allowed to a civilian.§

---

* Charge, &c., p. 22. † *Ibid.*, pp. 23, 47, 48.
‡ *Ibid.*, pp. 57, 58. § *Ibid.*, pp. 97, 99.

In coming to the case of Mr. Gordon, I will not repeat the language of the Lord Chief Justice, which I have given fully in another place.* It will suffice here to mention that his Lordship questioned the legality of his arrest by Mr. Eyre. It was an unjustifiable act to remove him from Kingston to Morant Bay. The constitution of the military tribunal was null and void. The evidence on which he was convicted was "inconclusive and utterly worthless," and much of it totally inadmissible in a properly constituted court of justice, honestly desirous of discharging its duty. Mr. Gordon was a man of peace, and had no intention, the very essence of crime, to produce an insurrection or of committing the offences of which he was accused. The judge concludes in these memorable words :—

"I CAN ONLY SAY THAT IT WAS AS LAMENTABLE A MISCARRIAGE OF JUSTICE AS THE HISTORY OF JUDICIAL TRIBUNALS CAN DISCLOSE." †

With these notable words ringing in their ears, the Grand Jury were in possession of ample reasons to justify sending the accused before a jury of their countrymen for full inquiry and decision. The charge failed in its purpose, and the arrested men were discharged.

Thus ended the Morant Bay tragedy, "IN A MISCARRIAGE OF JUSTICE." At all events the actors in it, while they may rejoice in their escape, must ever

---

* See *ante*, p. 106.   † Charge, &c., p. 154.

remain in the history of these events under the condemnation that fell from the lips of the highest
representative of the majesty and righteousness of
British law.

One happy result, however, of these discussions
has been to remove from the Statute Books of the
Colonies every Act which gave authority to the
Governors to proclaim martial law.* For the future,
though the prohibition, on necessity arising, is not
absolute, the Governor cannot be relieved from the
responsibility of taking such a step. He must himself be the judge whether the responsibility of pro-
claiming martial law is or is not greater than that of
refraining from doing so.

---

* Lord Carnarvon's Despatch to the Government of Antigua,
January 30th, 1867, printed 24th June, 1867.

CHAPTER XVI.

IT was with unfeigned satisfaction that the vast majority of the population of Jamaica, especially the coloured portion of it, received the nomination of Sir John Peter Grant to the Governorship of the Colony. As an old servant of the Indian Government, he was a man of great experience in the work of administration, and in all respects was admirably suited to deal with the grave questions it involved. His appointment was one of the last acts of Lord Russell's Ministry, and the result has more than justified the wisdom of the choice.

Sir John Peter Grant arrived at Kingston on Sunday, the 5th August, 1866, and on the next day was sworn in by Sir Henry Storks as Captain-General, and Governor-in-Chief, of the Island of Jamaica and its dependencies, with the usual ceremonial.

In his brief administration, Sir H. Storks had inspired all classes in the Colony with confidence and respect by his invariable kindness, firmness, and impartiality. He was well able to assure his successor "that perfect tranquillity prevailed throughout the Island of Jamaica, and persons of all parties seem disposed to afford the new Government every support and assistance." *

Governor Grant's first act was the appointment to his Council, in addition to his official staff, of three non-official members, all of whom had served under previous governors in the same capacity. The Government of Jamaica, under Sir J. P. Grant's direction, finally assumed the form of a Legislative Council of sixteen persons, consisting of the Governor at its head as President, and eight official and eight non-official members, all nominated by the Crown, forming one Legislative Chamber, and holding office at the Royal will and pleasure. All questions of revenue were to be introduced by the Governor alone, or by his authority.

The first time on which Governor Grant met in Session the new Council was on the 16th October, when, in a few words, he sketched the general character of the legislation he proposed to introduce.† He stated that in every department of administration there was much to be done ; and in no part of the work would be found a subject more important than a reform in the legal system of the Colony. The procedure of both civil and criminal courts, and the duties of the police, required the earliest attention. The actual police system was worthless, and the procedure of the courts, as it affected the poorer classes, was extremely bad, and gave no justice at all.

---

* Further Correspondence, August 10th, 1866, p. 94.

† Further Correspondence on the Affairs of Jamaica : Blue Book, dated July, 1867, p. 8.

Jamaica, in fact, **was, and always had been, a** genera-
tion behind **the mother country.** Too much, however,
must not be expected from legislative measures ; but
all bars and obstacles to progress must be removed.
The question of taxation also **required** immediate
notice. Retrenchment in expenditure was imperative.
The continual deficit must be checked.

But the new Governor's measures did not stop here.
He took in hand the appointment of a new and revised
system of magistracy. Public **works, such as the**
creation **of roads and** bridges, **were** placed **on a**
sounder basis, and so as to prevent **fraud** and pecula-
tion. **The reduction** of the Ecclesiastical Establishment
to a more moderate cost was essential, **with a view to**
its final abolition. **The great** question of elementary
education must be taken in hand, and, by a wise system
of grants-in-aid, the opening of schools must be encouraged **in all** parts **of the island, by** the various
Christian denominations, **and under their** direction.
The savings **on** the Ecclesiastical Establishment **could**
at once be devoted **to** this most important **object.***

These measures were quickly adopted. **Sustained**
by a wise, watchful, and vigorous administration, they
quickly changed the aspect of affairs, so that **by the**
beginning of the following year **Jamaica** was declared
never to have been in a more tranquil **state. The**
advent of Governor Grant was hailed everywhere
with acclamation. A general tone of hopefulness
took the place of depression and despondency. **During**

---

* **Blue Book, July,** 1867, **p.** 41.

the recent agitations there had been a loud outcry for a strong Government. It was now felt that the Government was in the hands of a strong man, armed, indeed, with unusual powers, but one whose rule was as just as it was strong, and as beneficent as it was wise. It was conducted, not in the interests of any class, but with a view for the benefit of all, labourers and planters alike. The lowliest subject of the Queen was made to feel that henceforth he would no longer be at the mercy of a corrupt Legislature or irresponsible magistrates, but under the immediate and vigorous protection of laws which govern the British Empire throughout the world. The way was cleared for the great Act of Emancipation to produce its richest fruits, and measures were actively taken to secure the rights and privileges it was passed to give.

On many of the subjects here referred to, previous to his departure for Jamaica from England, I had both the honour and pleasure of two or three long conversations with Sir John Peter Grant, and I have witnessed the execution of the plans we then discussed with the highest gratification. And if the publication of my letter, which drew so much attention to these subjects, was followed by dark moments, deep sorrows, and painful memories, it cannot but be a joy in my advanced years to see more than my most sanguine hopes realised in the present, by the encouraging success of the measures introduced by Sir John Peter Grant.

Jamaica is now inhabited by a flourishing, con-

tented, and happy peasantry. Peace and order everywhere prevail; crime has largely decreased. The
cultivation of the soil, the growth of numberless
homesteads and settlements, the secure possession
of their holdings by laborious and skilful labourers,
bear witness to the capacities and industry of a class
which, half a century ago, was held in hard and hopeless bondage.

The spread of education is assured by the establishment and prosperity of some 900 elementary schools,
all under Government inspection, but in the conduct
and improvement of which every section of the
Christian Church in the island bears a useful and
successful part. Ample provision has also been made,
under the Education Act, for the training of teachers,
in the richly endowed Mico Institution, in the Baptist
College (Calabar), Kingston, in the Moravian Male and
Female Institutions, and in the Government Female
Training College. New churches and chapels have been
built and are rising in every district, not only by the
vigorous and ever active exertions of the Dissenting
denominations, no longer treated as dissenters, but
as brethren, by the Episcopal Church, once called
" Established," now prospering in its liberty and self-
control, freed from State trammels, and occupying
its pulpits with a class of earnest, devoted, and pious
clergy it never before enjoyed. Congregations are
everywhere increasing in numbers and respectability.

Trade, too, has undergone many changes, but is
released from burdensome and obstructive charges.
The State expenditure is economised. Corruption

among officials is a thing of the past, and free access is enjoyed to all the markets of the world. And if sugar cultivation continues depressed from causes not local in their character, and has not shared to any great extent in the general revival, other exports more than replace it, and give opportunities of culture of desirable things which only tropical climes can produce.

Thus "The Morant Bay Tragedy," which at the time of its occurrence inflicted on the people such a burden of loss, lamentation, and woe, has, in the mysterious working of Divine Providence, proved to be laden with blessings, contributory to the well-being of a race "long despised and rejected of men." "The wilderness and the solitary place have been made glad, and the desert to rejoice and blossom as the rose. It shall blossom abundantly and rejoice, even with joy and singing."

LONDON :

PRINTED BY ALEXANDER AND SHEPHEARD,

27, CHANCERY LANE, W.C.

WORKS

BY EDWARD BEAN UNDERHILL, LL.D.

CHRISTIAN MISSIONS IN THE EAST AND
WEST in connection with the Baptist Missionary Society 1873

THE WEST INDIES. Their Social and Religious
Condition 1862

LIFE OF JAMES MURSELL PHILLIPPO. Missionary in Jamaica 1881

ALFRED SAKER. Missionary to Africa. A Bio-
graphy 1884

THE LIFE OF THE REV. J. WENGER, D.D.
Missionary in India and Translator 1886

THE DIVINE LEGATION OF PAUL THE
APOSTLE. An Essay 1889

LONDON: ALEXANDER & SHEPHEARD.

LIST OF WORKS

PRINTED AND PUBLISHED BY

ALEXANDER & SHEPHEARD.

BY DR. MACLAREN.

Crown 8vo, cloth boards, 5s., post-free.

CHRIST'S "MUSTS,"
AND OTHER SERMONS.

Author of "The Holy of Holies," "The Unchanging Christ," &c., &c.

" Dr. Maclaren is our ideal preacher."—*Expository Times.*

" Masterly, beautiful, inspiring."—*Methodist Recorder.*

" Felicitous exposition, rugged, intense eloquence, and beautiful illustration."
Word and Work.

" Forcible, clear, gracious, and suggestive."—*Presbyterian.*

" The words of a prophet, and we thank God for him."—*Christian Pictorial.*

Uniform with the above, price 5s., post-free.

THE WEARIED CHRIST,
AND OTHER SERMONS.

" Every succeeding volume of sermons by the Manchester 'prince of preachers' is eagerly anticipated, joyfully read, and thankfully preserved."
Sword and Trowel.

" They show the same wonderful fertility of apt and beautiful illustrations, the same exquisite use of language, the same direct heart-searching power which we are accustomed to find in all Dr. Maclaren's works."
Christian World Pulpit.

" For more than a quarter of a century he has held almost an unchallenged position as the prince of pulpit orators. . . . The back pews of Dr. Maclaren's church are in the nooks and corners of the earth."—*Methodist Times.*

" They are fully up to his old level, and are still unrivalled in their own manner."—*British Weekly.*

Crown 8vo, cloth boards, price 5s., post-free.

PAUL'S PRAYERS,
AND OTHER SERMONS.

"As striking and suggestive as any Dr. Maclaren has published. . . . The book is full of helpful thoughts."—*Christian World.*

"They are plain enough to be understood by the unlearned, and yet have sufficient richness and cogency to attract the most cultivated."
New York Observer.

Uniform with the above, 5s., post-free.

THE GOD OF THE AMEN,
AND OTHER SERMONS.

"The several sermons contained in this volume are replete with a keen spiritual insight, combined with an aptness of illustration and beauty of diction which cannot fail to both impress and charm the reader."—*Methodist Times.*

"It is a work of supererogation to commend to our readers a volume of sermons by one who may be styled the greatest living expositor."
Review of the Churches.

Uniform with the above, price 5s., post-free.

THE HOLY OF HOLIES.
A Series of Sermons on the 14th, 15th, and 16th Chapters of the Gospel by John.

"No British preacher has unfolded this portion of Scripture in a more scholarly style."—*North British Daily Mail.*

"It is great praise of any preacher to say that he is equal to handling these chapters."—*The American* (Philadelphia).

"Every sermon glows with unction, and shows intense power."
Methodist Recorder.

Uniform with the above, price 5s., post-free.

THE UNCHANGING CHRIST,
AND OTHER SERMONS.

"The work of a master of pulpit oratory."—*The Freeman.*

"Distinguished by the finest scholarship and most exquisite literary finish."
Christian Leader.

"Few preachers combine so many elements of effective pulpit address."
Independent.

ILLUSTRATIONS

From the Sermons of DR. MACLAREN.

EDITED AND SELECTED BY

JAMES HENRY MARTYN.

Containing over 500 beautiful and suggestive illustrations. With a Textual Index and an Alphabetical List of Subjects.

" Preachers and teachers will be glad to have in moderate compass these gems from the great preacher."—*Methodist Recorder.*

" Sunday-school teachers, especially of senior classes, will find this volume useful and suggestive."—*Sunday School Chronicle.*

ON THE BOOK OF JONAH.

A MONOGRAPH.

A CONTRIBUTION TO THE EVIDENCE OF ITS HISTORIC TRUTH.

By JOHN KENNEDY, M.A., D.D.

" Dr. Kennedy maintains his position with a breadth of knowledge, a clearness of insight, and a force of logic it is difficult to resist. . . . As the work of a man who has passed his fourscore, the monograph is remarkable."
Baptist Magazine.

" In discussing these points Dr. Kennedy has much to say which deserves a respectful hearing."—*British Weekly.*

PAUL AND CHRIST:

A PORTRAITURE AND AN ARGUMENT.

By J. M. CRAMP, D.D., Nova Scotia.

"It is a fair, orthodox presentation of the Apostle's life and chief teachings."—*Christian World.*

" The book is well worth a perusal."—*Sword and Trowel.*

BRITISH POLICY from SOCIAL, HOME,

and IMPERIAL POINTS of VIEW. By Colonel the Hon. ARTHUR PARNELL, Retired List of the Corps of Royal Engineers, Author of "The War of the Succession in Spain," "The Defences of the Kingdom," &c.

CONTENTS: Social Defects; Home Questions; Colonial and Foreign Relations; Our Eastern Empire; Defence Administration; Gibraltar and Spain.

JOSEPH MAZZINI. A Memoir by E. A. V.

With Two Essays by Mazzini: "Thoughts on Democracy" and "The Duties of Man."

"It would be cheap at a guinea."—*North British Daily Mail.*
"We doubt not that it will have an immense circulation."—*Echo.*
"Mazzini was one of the noblest patriots who ever wrought for the emancipation of peoples, and his life and work ought to be reverently studied."
Northampton Guardian.
"Written with a good deal of vivacity and evident knowledge of the subject."
Scotsman.

THE CONFLICT OF OLIGARCHY AND

DEMOCRACY. By J. ALLANSON PICTON, M.A.

"Not only contains a worthy programme of political action, but also expresses in language of singular beauty and felicity the teaching of a broad and fearless Christianity."—*Independent and Nonconformist.*

CHILDHOOD AND YOUTH. By JAMES

DUNCKLEY, Author of "A Saviour for Children," &c. Illustrated by E. GOODWYN LEWIS.

"Mr. Dunckley can instruct even while he amuses."—*Baptist Magazine.*
"Teachers may read this book with advantage."—*Sunday School Chronicle.*
"Mr. Dunckley's volume will take a high place among sermons to children.
British Weekly.

SACRED THEMES AND FAMOUS PAINT-

INGS. By Rev. DAVID DAVIES, Author of "Echoes from the Welsh Hills," "Christ Magnified," &c.

"If we were members of the Royal Academy we should give Mr. Davies a commission to describe our paintings and interpret their meaning."—*Freeman.*

DEVOTIONAL READINGS FOR THE

DAY of REST. By Rev. J. R. WOOD, Upper Holloway.

"The fruit of close and patient study of the Divine Word."—*Baptist Magazine.*